POISON TEA

A Sequel to *Two Dead on Crystal Creek*

By M. Sue Alexander

Poison Tea

FIRST EDITION 2021, USA
SUZANDER PUBLISHING

Book Cover by Christine Roszak

View M. Sue's Website and Facebook Page
www.msuealexanderbooks.com

Series Titles by Author

Resurrection Dawn 2014 Series
Book 1: Resurrection Dawn 2014 Book 2: The Christian Fugitive
Book 3: Rebels in Paradise   Book 4: Veil of Lies
Book 5: The Anointing   Book 6: Countdown to Justice
Book 7: All Rise   Book 8: Unlikely Suspect
Book 9: Lethal Snapshot   Book 10: Purgatory
Book 11: April Fool's Day   Book 12: Reign of Errors

Time of Jacob's Trouble
Book 1: The Four Horsemen   Book 2: Beast
Book 3: Witness Book 4: The Word
Book 5: Judgment   Book 6: Deceiver
Book 7: False Prophet Book 8: Satan
Book 9: The Image   Book 10: Jesus the Appearance

Independent Titles
Adam's Bones
Encounters of the God-Kind
The Forum
The Minister's Haunting
Tomorrow's Promise
Two Dead on Crystal Creek
Out of Time: The Vanderbilt Incident

1

Monday, October 24

I STAND AT MY BEDROOM window and remind myself that today is the best day of the rest of my life. Not that I worry how I will spend it. Or if today the Grim Reaper will visit me. Goodness, old age is far worse than joining my poor deceased husband in Heaven.

What am I thinking? I don't have time to die, Arthur. You'll just have to wing it up there until I join you sometime in the future.

The wind whispers through the trees; ripping colored leaves from the limbs and tossing them like confetti on my lawn. I've finally hired someone to mow for me since I can afford it, thanks to Arthur's forethought in taking out a $500,000 life insurance policy on himself and naming me as the beneficiary. I sigh, deep in speculation.

My ears perk up as I hear someone knocking on my back door.

I shrug on my terry-cloth robe and shove my size nine feet in my slippers, thinking no one in their right mind would come to my house at 6:15 a.m. in the morning. It has to be my neighbor, Lorene. She's the only friend that stops by at odd hours without calling first.

I hustle through the den as the wind whistles around the corners of my 1934 farmhouse. Seconds later, I tear open the kitchen door.

Lorene Perkins stands on the porch, frowning.

"Did you bring me flowers?" My lips wiggle.

"Not today." Lorene pushes past me as she enters my kitchen.

She's been my neighbor for decades. We have a common bond since she shares my grief. My Arthur and her Crawford died on the banks of Crystal Creek on the same day. Arthur was murdered by a Hit Man working for the Nashville Mafia while Crawford was scared to death and had a heart attack. But that was two years ago.

"I guess you want a cup of Joe first, before you explain why you've come to see me so early," I say, pattering into the kitchen.

Lorene releases a huge sigh. "That would be wonderful!"

"Well, catch your breath, dear, and sit down at the table," I order her. "I'll start the coffeemaker then you can tell me what's got you in such a dither this morning." I hope no one we know has died.

"Thanks." Lorene is shivering as she sheds her coat and parks it on the back of a chair at my breakfast-room table then sits down.

I stare at her a moment.

"What? You forgot how to make coffee?" she mutters.

I throw a hand. "Don't be so cute, I'm not in the mood." I disappear into the kitchen to divvy out the coffee grounds and add water to the coffeemaker. It's the simplest thing I will do today.

"Where's Pepper?" Lorene asks.

"He started throwing up mid-morning Saturday. I took him to the vet and left him for the weekend. He may have ingested some poison."

Lorene gave me the Yorkshire Terrier after Arthur died.

"I hope he'll be okay." Sadness crouches in my friend's face.

While the coffee drips I join Lorene at the table. "What's the matter, dear?" I try to be diplomatic. "Did something bad happen?"

"Yes." Tears cloud her eyes.

"Did someone die?" I ask, nearly holding my breath.

"Not yet." She hitches a breath.

"Someone we know is sick?" I feel like I'm pulling teeth out of a horse's mouth. I wait until Lorene is ready to share.

"It's my daughter, Heather. She has breast cancer."

I open my mouth and nothing comes out.

"I know, I was shocked, too." Lorene grabs my hand. "The doctor says the lump is still small and can be removed."

I nod as I hear the coffeemaker bubble out its contents.

"You want cream and sugar with your coffee?" I ask, not daring to project any idea that cancer has the power to take a life.

Lorene nods as she stares bleary-eyed at the wall.

I return to the table with two mugs dressed up in real cream and two teaspoons of pure honey. We're going to need our energy today.

We sip on our coffees in silence. I want to tell Lorene that everything will work out, that Heather will be fine. But life has taught me that humankind has little control over death. People get sick and die. Maybe Heather won't. I sure pray I am right.

"I have a new neighbor," I say, changing the subject.

"Who?" Lorene sets her mug on the table.

"She's pretty old, ninety-two," I tell her.

"Dorothy? We're pretty old. That doesn't tell me much about your new neighbor or where she lives," Lorene says.

"Her name is Alicia Anderton Colby and she's moved into Clyde's cabin behind my house," I explain. "She's from England."

"Have you visited her yet at the cabin?"

"No, she moved in two days ago, but I think we should."

"Well, yes. And take her a Welcome-Wagon gift."

I chuckle. "That organization went out decades ago," I declare. "People want their privacy. They don't want to be bothered."

"I know, but we still need to be neighborly, don't you think?"

I nod my head and sip on my coffee. The wall clock ticks off time behind me. I wait to see if Lorene has anything else she wants to say about Heather. She doesn't. The silence is almost painful.

"You're up earlier than usual," I tell her.

"There's another matter I wanted to share."

I wait for enlightenment.

She continues, "I thought I should come over and tell you about it in person," she says. "I didn't want you to read about it in the paper."

"About what?" I'm already upset over her statement.

"Did you receive the Columbia Gazette yesterday?"

Lorene is referring to the Sunday paper. "Yes, but I haven't read it yet. Is there something disturbing in it?" I eyeball her, concerned.

"No one we know died," Lorene repeats to abate my fears.

"Thank God for little favors!"

"A woman named Lorita Willems was murdered," Lorene reports. "She lives in Dickson, Tennessee—or did."

I think about what Lorene said.

"Was Lorita kin to Clyde Willems?"

"Yes, she is his half-sister. They share the same father."

"Oh." I wonder what her death has to do with me.

"I wanted to warn you that Butch may be calling you today."

"What? Whatever for?" Detective Lloyd Peters is not one of my favorite people, but he did help solve Arthur's murder and put that horrible Hit Man behind bars. "Tell me what you know, Lorene."

"Well, it says in the article that the police believe her death is connected to the three murders that occurred two years ago."

"To *my* Arthur's and *your* Crawford's?" I'm shocked.

"Apparently. Don't forget Clyde was murdered, too."

How could I possibly forget any of it? Nightmares remind me often that I am alone because evil exists in the world.

"Is there anything you're leaving out?" I ask Lorene.

"I don't think so. You can read the article for yourself."

"Okay, I will, but later. Are you hungry?"

"I could eat, what's for breakfast?" Lorene perks up.

"Whatever you want. I can still cook." Thank God!

Lorene leaves for home around eight a.m.

It's Monday so I'm busy with gathering dirty towels and my clothes to wash. I have a maid that comes every other Thursday to deep clean. On the fourth Thursday, I get my hair done at Gloria's.

And I still play Canasta with the girls every Friday from two to five p.m. at the Senior Citizen Center. My daughter Claire usually visits me on Tuesdays while her husband Ted plays golf with his buddies.

Mondays and Wednesdays are my "free" days.

Zoey Jackson comes by the house when she doesn't have a college class. I'm reminded that Donald, her grandfather, also was found dead two years ago. Zoey was a senior high-school student when she accompanied Butch and Ellie to Arthur's memorial service. I found out later that she was kidnapped by the Mafia and sold to a sheik in the Middle East, and that Butch and Ellie rescued her. I'm now paying for her college tuition. Gratefully, she does house chores for me.

Mid-morning, I go out the front door and check on the weather conditions. I see a Chevy truck driving up my way. *Butch.*

2

"MS. POWELL . . ." DETECTIVE PETERS says as he removes his cap, "is this a good time for us to talk?" There's a smirk on his unshaven face—nothing new under the sun. It's part of his persona.

"About the woman who was murdered in Dickson?" I let him know I'm not an ignorant idiot and keep abreast of current affairs.

"Cold outside, can we step inside?" he asks.

"Are you able?" I tease him about his choice of an English verb.

He chuckles. "Dorothy, you haven't changed a bit in two years!"

"Neither have you, Butch!" *In four decades*, I think to myself. I'll never forgive him for almost raping my Claire when she was in the ninth grade. Some things are unforgivable, God help me!

"Then you know Lorita Willems was murdered."

"I heard." We enter the front door of my house and proceed down the hall past my dining room and into the breakfast room.

He's docile as he follows, no doubt plotting his next move.

"Would you like a cup of Joe?" I recall my manners.

"No thanks, I'm tanked out." Butch glances into the den. "I see you've done some remodeling. New furniture. No wallpaper."

"My daughter says wallpaper is not fashionable. She sent over a painter and he took down all of it and painted everything beige."

I was happy with wallpaper and colored walls. I fought Claire about taking down the chicken-print paper in the kitchen. Arthur labored over that project so seeing it kept him in my memories.

"Everything looks great. Are you going to sell?"

"Nope. Not till I kick the bucket."

"Well, I hope that's not anytime soon," he chuckles, "but if you decide to sell and move, I'd like to put in an offer."

"Why?" Do I want him living in my house?

"Ellie and I are getting married Christmas Eve," he reveals. "I love your farm. And Ellie loves this house." He smiles sweetly at me.

I think the jerk is not all bad—at least, when he's with Ellie and under the influence of true love. "Sure, I'll let you know," I say.

"About Lorita . . ." he pulls out a chair at the breakfast table.

"How can I help you, Detective?" I'm all business now. In fact, it was me that took down the assassin that murdered Arthur. Mark Hagen is serving a life sentence in a Tennessee prison.

"How well do you know Alicia Colby?" he inquires.

"I don't know her at all. Jake, my mailman, told me she moved into Clyde's old cabin behind my house," I report. "Why?"

"I did some research and learned that Clyde left the cabin to Lorita," he said. "Apparently, she didn't want it—liked living in Dickson and worked at Cracker Barrel." He glares at me.

"Then how did Alicia come to live in the cabin?"

"That's what I want to know. Maybe you can talk to her."

I'm shocked. "You want me to spy on my new neighbor?" Butch has more confidence in my detective skills than he lets on.

"She's old and I don't want to upset her." He pats a pack of Lucky Strikes in his shirt pocket like he needs a smoke.

Really? He's upset me numerous times. "Are you going to deputize me so I can officially interrogate the elderly English lady?"

His lips form a pout. "That's not really necessary, Dorothy."

Good. I've aggravated him. Yet, I'm tickled at the idea.

"Okay, I'll do it. Lorene and I plan to pay our new neighbor a visit and take a housewarming gift," I reveal. "I'm curious, too."

"I know you are." Butch grins at me. "You're a good woman."

I don't know how to receive his compliment. Every bone in me creaks when I see him. I am not *good*. I am saved by God's grace.

Butch hands me his business card. "Call when you have news."

I see him to the front door and wave goodbye as he drives away. I can't wait to tell Lorene we have an assignment from the Columbia Police Department. We were born for *Undercover Work*.

I spend my morning plotting how to approach Alicia without seeming nosy. Lorene and I drive to town after lunch to purchase a nice gift for her. When we return to my house, we wrap the box of expensive European tea and get in my new red BMW.

I am so pumped over the idea of spying. My white curly hair is highlighted with a dark blood color. If I decide to get a facelift, I have the potential to look younger than my worn-out eighty-two years. And

I'm twenty pounds lighter than when I scattered Arthur's ashes on the farm. *Poor Lance.* Sadness attacks me as I think of my dead son.

"Earth to Dorothy!" Lorene snaps her fingers.

I'm operating on autopilot as I drive almost three miles up the gravel road toward the cabin. It's a lovely October afternoon with a light breeze scattering the colorful fallen leaves. The wheels of my BMW will be muddy from deep puddles filled by last night's cold rain. I don't care. A carwash will restore its glory. I realize Lorene is saying something to me. "What?" I focus my blue eyes on my friend.

"What's the plan? Are we just going to drive up to the cabin and park? Then knock on the front door?" Lorene queries me.

"No other choice. Alicia's phone number is unlisted."

"Do you think she knows how to use a cell phone?"

"I imagine, but we can ask her," I reply. "Remember, keep your questions low-key. We don't want to appear like we're spying."

"But we are," Lorene declares. "Does it bother you?"

"Nope. We are acting in an official capacity," I declare. "Right out of the horse's mouth. We'll be discreet, I promise."

I'm getting excited as we grow closer to the cabin. Wouldn't matter if Butch asked me to question Alicia, I would have anyhow. It's my nature to be curious. "You can still back out," I tell Lorene.

"Not on my life." She tugs at her too-tight leather jacket.

I park in front of the cabin.

"I see lights on inside," Lorene whispers.

"You don't have to whisper, she can't hear you," I say, smiling at the prospect of meeting someone new in our neighborhood.

We stand on the porch landing looking at one another, wondering if we should knock. "I'll do it," Lorene volunteers.

But the door comes open before she has the chance.

Suddenly, I feel tongue-tied. Lorene gushes, "We're your closest neighbors, so we wanted to stop by and welcome you to Tennessee."

Alicia Anderton Colby assesses us like a spider surveying a perspective fly. "May we come in?" I find my voice.

"And who may I say is calling?" Alicia holds to the door.

"I'm Dorothy Powell. I live in the farmhouse you pass by every time you drive to the cabin," I explain. "This is Lorene Perkins." I grab her elbow. "She lives three miles down the road from me as you drive toward Columbia. We brought you a welcome gift."

I hand Alicia the wrapped package containing tea bags.

"Thank you." She appears uncertain. "I suppose it is safe for you to come inside. I've had prowlers the last few nights."

I love her English brogue. It's chic.

"Really?" I step inside with Lorene following. "Did you report the incident to the Columbia Police Department?"

"No, my great niece recently died—you probably read about it in the Columbia Gazette," Alicia says. "Please. Be seated, ladies."

The transformation of Clyde's cabin is remarkable. The pine floors have been refinished and colorful rugs are scattered about. The log-cabin walls have been sprayed with a varnish and original artwork displayed on them. A fire is set in the hearth, glowing warmly.

"I love what you've done to the cabin," I comment.

"Lorita did this before I moved to the States." Alicia continues to stand a bit wobbly. "Would you like a cup of hot tea? I'm chilled."

"That sounds perfect," I say.

"Open your gift," Lorene adds, "then we'll have tea."

Alicia sits down on a two-seater plush sofa the color of a sunset. She appears delighted at the brand of tea we've given her. Peppermint, and from her hometown of Lancashire, England. We didn't know that when we purchased the tea, but it did not hurt our cause.

"Make yourself comfortable, ladies, while I'll fix our beverages."

While Alicia is busy in the kitchen, Lorene leans close and whispers, "I like her already. I don't think it's right to spy on her."

"You don't have to, Lorene. I'll do the talking." It is the wrong time to let guilt defeat me. I believe Alicia will share her heart with us because she wants to mentor our friendship. Time will unfold truth.

We sit up straight as Alicia appears in the doorway with a silver tray of teacakes with condiments for the hot beverage. The cups and saucers are an expensive porcelain, and the silver spoons are polished to perfection. Alicia comes from wealth, so why live in a cabin?

We nibble on the teacakes and drink our tea, all the while I contemplate how to interview Alicia. She appears fragile and sad from the loss of her great niece. No sunlight had touched her delicate white skin, a network of age lines. But her small eyes are a burnt green and radiate still-vibrant intelligence. She is still quite healthy.

"Have you always lived in Maury County?" Alicia inquires.

"We both have for decades," Lorene answers for us.

"How did you know I was from Lancashire?"

"Lucky guess," I reply. "What's your story?"

Alicia blinks back tears. "I'm not sure you have the time."

"We do!" Lorene and I simultaneously reply.

3

"WELL, THAT WAS INTERESTING," Lorene quips to me as I drive us to town. No better time than now to report what we learned about Alicia Colby while the facts are fresh on our minds. "She's nice."

"Yes, she is, and I like her." A bit of guilt assaults me for what I'm about to do. I was never a tattle-tale-type of person. Until now.

Butch's office is located on Third Street in one of the three Columbia Police precincts. I park in VISITORS then we get out of my BMW and go inside. Hank is on desk duty and calls up to Ellie.

"She says Detective Peters will see you," Hank tells me.

"Thank you." I smile sweetly at him.

Lorene elbows me. "Stop flirting, he's married."

I laugh, "And two decades younger than me." We step into the elevator that takes us up to the Second Floor. The door to Butch's office comes open as he looks both ways down the hall.

"Did a criminal just escape your clutches?" I tease him.

"No, come on in," he says, not explaining his behavior.

"Hi, Ellie. I heard you were tying the knot on Christmas Eve." I jab a thumb at Butch. "Or is he tying you up and making you marry him?" I'm so on a roll this afternoon, a detective after my own heart.

"Cute!" he scoffs as we enter his office and he slams the door.

Lorene has no comment. I think she's afraid of him. I'm not.

"Sit, ladies." He fiddles with a cigarette lighter. I'm aware that Ellie doesn't permit him to smoke. I love the idea he's henpecked.

"We talked to Alicia Colby," I inform him.

"And . . .?" he rolls his left hand.

"And, she's super nice," Lorene adds, her lips loosening.

"She's from Lancashire, England," I pipe in.

"Tell me something I don't know." He rocks back in his chair.

"She's royalty," I add. "From the historic Andertons' family line. James Anderton was born in 1542. His cousin was related to Queen Elizabeth I. She's a devout Catholic, like all the other Andertons."

Butch sits up straight in his chair. "Did she say how she came to live in the states?" His hands are clasped on his shiny desk.

"No," I reply. "That information will take another visit."

He smirks. "You're wasting my time, ladies. I don't care a whit about Miss Colby's British heritage, I want to know how she ended up owning Clyde's old cabin. What's so valuable about the property?"

"Well, the cabin is quite nice now," Lorene chimes in. "The floors have been refinished and Alicia's furniture and artwork are superb. You should sit with her sometimes and have a cup of tea."

Butch looks like a wounded attack dog, not appreciating our remarks or that we are worth his time or the city's money—not that we're paid informants. I need to clarify our purpose in spying.

"I know it isn't much, Lloyd," I enter the conversation. "But we need to gain Alicia's confidence before she tells us her family secrets."

He looks longingly at me. "You're right. Go spy some more."

Lorene stiffens. "I prefer to call it neighborly curiosity."

"Call it anything you want, Ms. Perkins, just get me the information." He gets up and opens the door. "Good day, ladies."

We're standing out in the hall in front of the elevator when I look at Lorene and say, "Did you feel like he kicked us out?"

"Absolutely!" The elevator doors invitingly part.

We get on and descend a story to the lobby.

"I think we should do some digging on our own," I suggest. "Let's take a drive to Dickson tomorrow and talk to some of Lorita's friends." I'll bypass Detective Peters and solve this murder mystery.

"Isn't Claire coming over tomorrow?" Lorene asks as we exit the building. We get into my car and drive two blocks.

"I'll check with her. Are you free to accompany me?"

"Well, I need to drive to Kentucky and check on Heather sometime this week. I guess I could do that on Wednesday."

"Okay then, I'll let you off at your house and pick you up tomorrow morning at nine a.m. We'll stop at Cracker Barrel for breakfast." Butch told me where Lorita had worked. "Okay?"

"Fine." Lorene yawns.

I suppose detective work is exhausting to most people. Not me, it just gets my juices going. If I could go back sixty years, my path to fame would involve joining the police force rather than teaching a bunch of kids that aren't interested in learning. I smile at the idea.

The afternoon passes uneventfully, my mind whirring like wind that has begun to kick up again, chasing after a potential thunderstorm. For supper, I warm up some vegetable soup and look for a Hallmark movie on TV I haven't seen, wondering if it truly exists at my age.

Claire doesn't answer her cell phone, and it worries me. Do parents ever quit thinking their children are their responsibility? I won't. Not ever. My Claire is a special jewel in my life, and I will forever hang her around my neck like a precious necklace.

Goodness, I'm sentimental!

Aw life! How it changes day by day. Never a dull moment in my sphere. *Oh Arthur, I wish you were here to see what good I'm doing.*

4

Tuesday, October 25

PLANS BEST CRAFTED ARE sometimes sabotaged. So, it was to be on Tuesday. Lorene called my cell number at 6 a.m. and woke me.

"Are you up?"

"I am now, Lorene. Is something wrong?"

"I can't go with you to Dickson today," she gushes.

"Are you sick?" I climb from my bed and shiver, hoping my heat hasn't crashed. I stumble to a chair and grasp my housecoat.

"No, Heather phoned me not fifteen minutes ago, crying. She will have emergency surgery this Friday. I have to be with her."

"You're going to Kentucky for the rest of the week?" I could not believe our bad luck. Just when we were on a roll to solve a crime. Maybe the Grim Reaper is at work again, God help us.

"I'm sorry, Dorothy, I know you were counting on me to go with you to Dickson today. Maybe one day next week," she says.

"Don't you worry about that," I say, disappointed enough for both of us. "I have plenty to keep me busy today. God is good and He will take care of Heather. Have faith, dear." I feel empathy for her.

"Thank you." I hear a sigh. "You're a good friend, Dorothy."

"I hope so," I say. "Tell Heather I'll pray for her."

"I will, I'm leaving in thirty minutes."

"Are you driving yourself?"

"No, my son Sam is taking me," she replies.

"Good. Be safe, both of you." Sam is a brave firefighter.

The phone clicks off at the other end. I stand in my robe staring at it then toss it on my unmade bed like it's the enemy. Then it rings again. O Lordy! What else can go wrong with today?

"Hello."

"Mama, it's me."

"Claire! Tell me you are all right and Ted is fine, as well as the children." I shake in my slippers at the idea of the Grim Reaper.

"What's wrong, Mama. You sound hysterical."

"No, I'm okay, Claire. What's up?"

"Did you forget I was coming over today?"

"No, I tried phoning you last night to tell you Lorene and I were taking an excursion, but you did not answer. Then I fell asleep in the recliner and did not wake up until after eleven," I reveal.

"I shut it off to watch a movie with Ted."

"What if I'd had an emergency?" I blurt out.

"Did you?" she asks, sounding a bit irritated.

"No, so none of it matters now."

"Mama. You are not making a shred of sense this morning. Are you positive you're fine?" Claire asks. "Should I be worried?"

"No, no, it's just—never mind. What time are you coming over?" I inquire. I will not tell her about my detective assignment.

"I'll pick you up around eleven, and we'll go out to lunch."

"That sounds fantastic!" I'm not happy about cancelling my trip to Dickson. There's no time like the present for revelation.

"I hear there's a new seafood restaurant in Columbia."

"We'll go anywhere you choose." Food is not my priority right now as I try to reinvent the day to achieve my personal goals.

"Okay, Ted can't find his new tie, I have to go."

My daughter has hung up on me without my saying a proper goodbye. Theodore. She loves him more than me.

That's silly, I tell myself. Love has many facets. *Now I'm a poet?*

I am pattering through the den with the phone dangling in one hand and my dirty towel and washrag in the other when it rings.

I stop in my tracks and stare at the thing.

It continues to ring. "Hello!" I drop the towel and give in.

"It's Alicia. I had visitors last night."

"You have more relatives living here?" I don't understand.

"No, it was another prowler," the English woman says.

"Did someone break into your cabin?" I'm startled.

"No, but they left me a note. Can you come over? Now?"

"Of course, I can. I need to put on clothes then I'll be right over. Don't open the door to anyone but me." Help is on the way.

Suddenly, I feel optimistic. In the eons of time, it appears a moment of opportunity opens up that might come only one time in a thousand for answers to be revealed. Maybe God knew today would be better if I did not go to Dickson. I am free to help Alicia Colby.

After dumping my dirty towel and rag in the laundry room, I retrace my steps to the bedroom and hurriedly dress in a pair of blue slacks and a warm golden-weave sweater. The house feels cold—which means my heat is struggling to warm my space. I'll need to call a repair man before the day is out. Grabbing my BMW fob from my purse, I lock my kitchen door as I exit and click open the car door.

It's freezing outdoors after a cold front passed through, the temperature feeling in the twenties. Southern Tennessee might get an early snow this year. Global warming in reverse. Isn't that dandy?

It takes me only six minutes to drive down the gravel road to the cabin. In my mind, the log house will always belong to Clyde. I understand why Lorita did not choose to live there. It's stuck in the middle of thick woods, mostly hardwoods. One would wonder if the prowlers were forest elves. I am being silly this morning.

I sigh and wish I'd taken the time to perk more coffee and eat a muffin as my stomach rumbles like a truck with a bad. axle.

Oh well . . . it is what it is.

Alicia opens the door as soon as she sees me park in front of the cabin. I dash inside and she closes and locks the door behind me.

"Oh, thank you for coming, Dorothy." She tightly hugs me. "I was so frightened." The old woman appears thinner than yesterday.

"No problem, we're good friends now." I hug her back. "Do you by any chance have coffee made?" I feel desperate for a cup of Joe.

"I have instant," she replies, her burnt-green eyes coming alive. "Or I could make you a delicious cup of hot tea with honey."

"I need the caffeine; it's been an unusual morning."

"Well, you just sit down and rest while I make you a strong cup of Folgers to get you going. Nothing like it in your cup."

I chuckle. She's seen an old movie with an ad for that brand of coffee. The fire is crackling in the hearth and glows happily. Somehow light makes me feel better, more joyful over my day. I smell the coffee.

"There!" She brings my cup on a tray with cream in a small vessel and sugar in a covered sugar bowl. "Enjoy!" She's added a muffin.

I doctor my coffee and take a healthy sip. "Thank you, Alicia. You've taken care of me, now let me take care of you." I look at her.

"Oh, the note . . ." she removes it from her apron pocket. "I found it on the front landing this morning when I let Susan out."

"Who's Susan?" I ask, munching on the English muffin.

"My Persian cat. She sleeps in my bedroom most of the day and prowls at night. She's a bloodthirsty animal that bays at the moon."

I laugh. Alicia is witty. Her mind is still sharp. She hands me the folded note and I open it to read the contents. LEAVE OR YOU WILL GET HURT, it says in capital block letters. I give it back.

"Why does anyone want me to leave?" she queries. "Is there something hidden in this cabin somebody desperately wants?"

"I don't know, but there must be a reason," I speculate. "I think you should call Detective Peters and invite him over. Tell him about your prowlers and show him the note," I suggest. "Be safe, dear."

"Okay, but I don't want to be alone today," she says.

"Then come home with me. My daughter Claire is coming over around eleven this morning and we can all go to lunch in Columbia," I invite her. "Have you visited our quaint town?"

"Just driven through when a taxi brought me from the airport." She suddenly sobs. "I never had the chance to speak to Lorita. The police were at her apartment when I arrived in Dickson." She removes a handkerchief from her apron pocket and blows her nose.

"I'm so sorry, her death must have been a terrible shock."

"Yes, and Lorita never told me the real reason she did not want to live in Clyde's cabin," Alicia continues to reveal interesting details.

"How did you get your furniture delivered from England?" I inquire, finishing off my coffee and muffin. Details, please.

"They came by ship and Lorita arranged for them to be delivered to the cabin two weeks ago. Shortly after Clyde passed, she phoned and asked me if I'd like to live out the rest of my life in America. I said yes, and she got the ball rolling—as you Americans say."

Her smile was endearing.

"Well, I'm certainly glad you came," I declare. "And don't you worry a hair, we will take good care of you now that Lorita is—"

"Gone," Alicia finishes my sentence, sniffling as tears bubble in her eyes again. "We didn't often see one another, but we're family."

"I understand. Family is important. Family bonds are strong and usually unbreakable." I say usually because some people I know do not value family. Like Zoey Jackson's father, serving time in prison.

"We need to go now, Alicia. A young friend of mine usually stops by the house around ten," I say. I also forgot to cancel Zoey's visit.

What is wrong with me? Am I becoming senile?

5

CLAIRE IS LATE, IT'S already eleven thirty. Alicia is seated on the sofa perusing a *Better Homes and Garden* magazine while I return some phone calls. "I need to pick up Pepper after we have lunch," I tell her as I stand in the open archway between the den and my breakfast room.

"No problem, I'm happy to tag along."

"Can I get you anything? A cup of tea or a cold beverage?"

Alicia lays the magazine aside and hobbles to her feet.

"No, I'm fine. Who's Pepper?"

"My terrier, he came down sick this past Saturday so he's been recuperating at the vet's all weekend. "You should get a dog."

"Puppies and cats fight," she says. "Susan wouldn't like it."

I motion for her to sit down as I choose Arthur's recliner, the only furniture in the den that's not new. "A big dog roaming the yard will alert you to visitors." I think of her prowler and what danger it poses.

"Maybe after my Persian passes, I will," she comments.

As I contemplate her response, my conscience bothers me.

"Is something wrong, Dorothy?" Her gaze traps my face.

"I need to confess something."

"I can't imagine what," she says with a slight smile.

"Detective Peters asked me to spy on you."

Alicia's expression reflects surprise.

"Does he think I murdered Lorita?"

"No, nothing like that—Butch just wants to know more about your past life, and if there's anything that will shed light on Lorita's death." I stall a moment. "Butch is a nickname for Detective Peters."

"Oh." She gathers her small wrinkled hands in her lap, head downcast as she considers my statement. Then she looks up.

What? It's my inaudible expression that prompts an answer.

"I know about her deceased husband's association with the Mafia," Alicia confesses. "Lorita told me all about his involvement with them over the phone soon after he died." Her eyes wither with speculation. "Do you think they killed her? If so, why now?"

"Remind me, how long ago did he pass?"

"Joseph? It was a good five years ago," she replies.

"There's a lot we still don't know," I suggest, and wonder what secrets Butch is keeping from me. "The news article in the Columbia paper did not give details regarding how Lorita was murdered."

I wait for more info, hoping Alicia will share more details.

"I wish Detective Peters would talk to me in person." She gets up as someone knocks on my kitchen door. "I have nothing to hide."

"That will be my daughter, Claire." I rise to my feet, concerned that Alicia appears nervous. She's truly afraid of something. What?

Claire lets herself into the kitchen, since I failed to lock the door. "Good morning, Mama!" Her gaze settles on my new friend.

"Oh, this is Alicia Colby, she lives in Clyde Willems' old cabin," I explain as I approach Claire and hug her. "How are you today?"

"I'm fine." She extends a handshake to my new neighbor.

"Good to meet you, Claire," Alicia says in a shaky voice.

"I'm glad Mama has a friend living close to her," Claire states. "One cannot be too careful these days." She shrugs off her coat. "It's brutal outdoors today. I think we might even get our first snowfall."

"Alicia has a prowler. Her note confirms it," I say.

"What note?" My daughter inquires.

"Let's not get into all *that* now," Alicia intervenes.

Evidently, Alicia prefers to keep the prowler between us.

Claire drops her purse on the table behind the sofa. "Is this new, Mama?" She rubs the slender table's shiny wood surface.

"Yes, it is," I reply. Except for Arthur's recliner, I'd replaced all my den furniture after the paper was dismantled and the walls painted a dull beige color. "Are we ready to go?"

"I'll drive," Claire offers. "Alicia can sit up front with me."

"Okay." I never turn down a chauffeur.

"I'll use the facilities first," Alicia tells us.

I point to the hallway on the other side of the den.

"Take your time, we'll wait for you right here."

Ten minutes later, Claire is driving us to Columbia in Ted's Mercedes Benz. "What is your husband doing today?" I query Claire.

"He's home with a cold, Mama."

"Oh, dear! I pray you didn't bring that virus to us!"

I can tell Claire did not appreciate my comment.

"No, Mama, I've kept a safe distance from him."

We exit the house. Alicia is awfully quiet in the passenger seat, watching the countryside as the car zooms toward town way too fast.

"Alicia is from Lancashire, England." I lean forward so Claire can hear me better. "Her great-great somebody was related to Queen Elizabeth the First," I reveal. "This is her first visit to America and she intends to stay until . . ." *death do us part*. I won't admit it verbally.

Alicia chuckles. "I know that ol' saying, Dorothy."

"Sorry," I apologize, sitting back as I take a huge breath.

"I came to America at my great niece's request," Alicia explains to Claire. "Clyde left the cabin to her, and she didn't want it."

"I see." Claire roars over hills and threads through valleys at warp speed. Fifteen minutes later, we pass the speed sign and slow down.

"Her niece was recently murdered," I add to Alicia's remarks.

Claire glances over at her, lips parted with surprise. "The woman from Dickson that was recently murdered is your niece?"

"Yes, her mother married my grandson. It's quite tragic. Lorita is—was in her late forties. A wonderful person who would never hurt a fly. I'd like to get my hands on her killer," Alicia says with as much purpose as what rises in me as I think of solving the heinous crime.

I smile to myself. She may be old but she hasn't lost her spunk.

Claire pulls into Troy's Seafood and Steak, the newest restaurant downtown on the square. The owner is a chef from New York.

We climb out of Ted's car and Claire locks the doors.

"I've been wanting to try this restaurant since I read about in the Nashville *Tennessean*," Claire says as we approach the front door.

It's early, so we easily get seats at a table overlooking an enclosed garden area with a flowing fountain. "This is lovely," Alicia comments.

Troy comes over to greet us. "Good afternoon, ladies. Can I start you out with a complimentary cocktail since this is your first visit?"

"How did you know?" Claire looks up at him.

"I always remember pretty women." His smile is radiant.

He's flirting with Claire, I tell myself. *Ted better watch his p's and q's.*

"That's very sweet of you, Troy," Alicia says. "An old woman like me rarely gets compliments. But there was a time in my earlier years."

"I bet there were a lot of admirers." He leans over and whispers something in Alicia's ear that promotes a grin and flushes her cheeks.

"I don't suppose you're sharing secrets," I say.

"No, ma'am. For Alicia's ears only."

As he walks away, I comment, "He'll sell a lot of food and wine."

"He sure will. He's mighty good looking," Claire comments, then looks at me. "Mama, please don't tell Ted I said that."

I zip my lips with a finger, tickled over her comment. She still loves Theodore, but a woman can't help looking sometimes.

"Well, let's peruse the menu and decide on an entrée, my treat," Claire says as the Perrier and laminated menus arrive at our table.

As we leave Troy's I feel satisfied. "The Lobster Thermador was to die for," I comment, then notice the horror on Alicia's face.

"I'm sorry, wrong verb." I swallow my embarrassment.

"It's okay, Dorothy," she admits, "I'm a little jumpy these days."

"I can only imagine." Claire clicks the fob to open the car doors.

We swing by the Vet's to pick up Pepper. My dog is rambunctious and all over me in the backseat. He's so happy to see me. Pets love their owners no matter their shortcomings. *Oh, Arthur!* I wish you were still here to share this moment. My thoughts are private.

Zoey Jackson is sitting on my front porch steps as Claire drives up to the house. "Oh, Lordy! Stop the car, Claire."

I tumble out the door, Pepper yelping as he leaps from the seat and runs after me like an attack dog. The ferocious little bugger. I gather him in my arms to protect Zoey. She waves from the porch.

"I'm sorry, Zoey, when you didn't show up at ten, I assumed you weren't coming," I tell her as I approach. I'm paying her college tuition so she usually cleans for me or does chores every Tuesday—whatever I ask her to do. She is a beautiful young lady with great promise.

"No problem, Ms. Powell," she replies. "Sorry about the mix up. I'll walk around the house and meet you at the backdoor."

I climb back in the car with Pepper and Claire drives to the shed and parks in the gravel. Zoey is shivering as we enter the house through the kitchen door. Alicia is a step ahead of me, and I can tell our trip tired her out. Ted phones Claire as soon as we're safely inside.

"I'd better get this." Claire walks into the den.

We all shed our coats and hang them on the five-prong wooden coat tree standing in the corner of the breakfast room. Claire's conversation with Ted is short-lived. Her expression reflects worry.

"What is it?" I inquire.

"I need to go home now," Claire informs me. "Ted feels worse and he wants me to drive him to the clinic," she explains.

"No problem." I give her a hug. "Try to stay well, dear."

"I will, Mama. And Alicia, Zoey, you both stay well and safe, too."

"Nice to meet you, Claire. We'll be fine. We'll take care of each other," Alicia says and her statement makes me feel really good.

I ask Zoey to strip the sheets and put in a load of laundry then vacuum and dust the den and kitchen area. She has a key to my house so she can leave after that. "Are you taking me home?" Alicia asks.

"First, I want you to take an excursion with me," I say.

"Where are we going?"

"Let me surprise you."

"Okay! I love surprises!"

6

PEPPER CANNOT GO WITH us on our excursion, so I let him out to pee then lock him in his crate. He'll sleep most of the afternoon.

"Where are we going?" Alicia asks as I turn north, the wrong direction from Columbia. She shivers a bit so I turn up the heat.

"Like I said, it's a surprise." I don't want to alarm her, or worry her about what I am about to do. Something I deem necessary.

The drive to Dickson takes forty-five minutes, a much shorter trip as the crow flies, but hills and valleys slow me down. I look over and see Alicia squeezing her hands together. The unknown bothers her.

"Okay, we're going to Cracker Barrel in Dickson and talk to some of Lorita's work buddies," I finally reveal the truth. "Maybe she said something to them that would help us understand why she died."

Alicia's head slowly turns toward me. "I'm not sure I'm up to that," she admits. "Her death is so fresh on my mind."

I pat her cold hand. "I'm sorry, dear, but since you are Lorita's great aunt, I thought your presence would open up a conversation."

"With someone who might give us a clue about why she died." Alicia nods. "So, I'm the bait." She nervously chuckles.

I laugh hard. "I'm so sorry, Alicia. This is truly mean of me."

"No, I'm all in," she says. "What are friends for?"

"Are you sure? We can still turn around and go home," I offer.

"No, to catch a fish, you need good bait."

I release a sigh, feeling minimally better about my ruse.

Cracker Barrell is virtually empty at three in the afternoon. Only a few coffee drinkers enjoying desserts sit at the scattered tables. Their laptops are open so I suspect they're engaged in conversations.

We take a seat at a table near the kitchen, my request.

The first server that comes to our table to take our order looks worn out. He probably took care of the luncheon crowd and is counting the minutes before he clocks out and goes home.

"What for you gals?" he wearily asks.

"I'll have a glass of cold tea," Alicia replies.

"Same here for me—oh, George!" I note his nametag. "Did you know Lorita Willems?" I palm at Alicia. "This is her great aunt."

George's eyes are a dull gray and huge and I note a glassy tear. "I sure did, she was a real sweetheart. We were sad she died."

"Murdered," I correct him. "Did you ever notice anyone coming in the restaurant who gave her grief?" Get right to the point.

"Not that I recall, but you should talk to Tina, they were close."

"Is Tina here?" I query.

"No, her day off."

"Any way we can phone Tina?" Alicia speaks.

"Well, since you're Lorita's great aunt, I suppose it would be alright if I gave you her cell phone number. But keep it on the quiet."

Alicia zips her lips with a finger, signaling she will.

We drink most of our cold tea and leave the restaurant. "Do you want me to call Tina?" I inquire as soon as we are seated in the car.

"If you don't mind, since I don't own a cell phone."

"We should get you a burner, in case you're away from the cabin and need to make a call," I say. "My gift to you. Okay?"

"Does it really burn?" She is puzzled.

"No, it's a phone with minutes to talk, disposable," I explain.

"Okay, sounds interesting, if you teach me how to use it."

"Easy as eating pie," I reply with a grin as I start the motor.

Tina is home and we've been invited to visit her. She lives in a duplex a few streets off Main Street. I see her standing on the porch waving as I drive up and park my BMW on the street.

We open the car doors and climb out. A brisk cold wind is stirring the bushes. Clouds above are thick and dingy. It feels darker than four fifteen. The weather is turning nasty fast, and that concerns me.

"Looks like a storm is brewing," Alicia notes.

"We won't stay long, I promise. Then we'll head on home."

Alicia shivers as she clutches her arms to her waist.

Tina is in her early forties, divorced. She's still an attractive woman, but wear-and-tear are deposited under her droopy hazel eyes. Her hair is the color of a sunset, a bit too bloody for my liking.

We approach her with anticipation.

"Thank you for seeing us, Tina," I say. "As I said on the phone, I'm Dorothy Powell and this is Alicia Colby, Lorita's great aunt from England. We were hoping Lorita told you some of her secrets."

"Good to meet you both, come inside." Tina opens the door to her compact living room and we step indoors. The room is tidy and clean. "Can I get either of you a beverage?" she inquires.

"Not for me," Alicia replies, "I had cold tea at Cracker Barrel. George was very kind and gave us your phone number."

"Against the rules, but that's George!" Tina throws a hand.

We take a seat, me on the sofa, and Alicia settles into the soft cushion of a wingback. Tina fills an antique rocker with her skinny frame that looks like it has also had some wear and tear over the years.

"Secrets, huh?" Tina rolls her eyes in thought. "The last time I spoke with Lorita, she'd received a package of tea from a relative." She leans forward. "It was very expensive, I recall. Peach."

"What relative?" I ask.

"I'm Lorita's only living relative!" Alicia exclaims.

"She did not say," Tina adds.

"I did not send Lorita a gift of tea, so who did?" Alicia's dark eyes flecked with green exhibit fear and questions alight on me.

"We should talk to the coroner and find out what caused Lorita's death," I decide. "I'm thinking the tea was laced with poison."

"Really?" Tina gushes. "Around here, a person takes a bullet."

I don't know how to respond to her statement.

"Anything else you recall about conversations with my niece?" Alicia inquires. "We really want to know what happened to her."

"She did mention a prowler, someone in her garden area in back of her apartment," Tina recalls. "I told the police about it."

"I've recently had a prowler, too," Alicia says.

"Did Lorita describe her prowler?" I inquire.

"Only that he was huge and black. She didn't see his face," Tina replies. "I hope this is helpful. Are you authorized to investigate?"

"I am," I say. "Detective Lloyd Peters asked for my help."

Tina frowns. "Are you deputized?"

"No, just making a few inquiries into Lorita's death," I answer.

Alicia looks at me. "We should go, the wind's picking up."

I hear windows rattle and distant thunder rumbling like a heavy train lumbering along its tracks. I despise driving in the rain.

"Thank you, Tina, you've been helpful." We all stand up.

"Drive carefully," Tina warns us.

"We will." I thank her and we leave.

Alicia sits in silence as I maneuver Highway 46 heading south. We are both speculating about the gift of tea and who sent it.

"What's our next move?" Alicia suddenly blurts out.

"I need to report to Detective Peters what we've learned today."

She nods. Rain blasts the car's windshield.

I add, "By now, Butch has read the coroner's report and knows the cause of Lorita's death," I expound like a true detective. "But first, we need to get home before this weather blows us off the road."

It's a bumpy drive home. And very dark.

We're at my house by six fifteen, and I insist that Alicia spend the night with me. The storm outside is roaring. She agrees that sleeping alone in the cabin on a stormy night is not appealing.

"Will Susan be okay alone tonight?"

"Yes, she's a hearty breed and has plenty of food and water. She's trained to use the cat-litter box," Alicia assures me.

We have warmed leftovers for supper, a beef casserole I removed from the freezer before we left for Columbia. It's thoroughly thawed.

After supper, we hover together in the den, trying to ignore the whipping wind and hard rain beating on my roof. It's so dark outdoors I think the End of Days has arrived and God's light has gone out in the universe. The TV endlessly drones on. The electricity crashes at nine, so I light candles in the den. "Thank God, we're safe."

"What do you do on a night like this?" Alicia inquires.

"I usually read a novel or a magazine." I hop up from the recliner and gather several from the basket situated at one end of the sofa.

I can tell Alicia's about to cry. My heart goes out to her.

"I could heat water over the gas eye and make you tea," I offer.

"No, thank you. After what I've learned today. . ."

"Oh, the poison tea—I understand." The raw truth for a dark moment in time chills my bones. "Are you sleepy yet?"

"What time is it?"

"Early still, but I'm weary." I widely yawn. "First, I need to put clean sheets on the bed in the guestroom, you want to help me?"

"Sure." Alicia slowly rises to her feet and groans.

"I know, ol' Arthur eating at your bones."

We both laugh as we shuffle toward the bedroom wing.

The task of making up the bed doesn't take long. I tuck my new neighbor in bed and cover her. "Goodnight and sweet dreams."

"Thank you, Dorothy." Alicia closes her eyes.

She looks like a porcelain doll lying so still. Her lips are bubbling in sleep by the time I walk to the door and turn around.

I hope she's going to be all right, I think to myself.

"Goodnight, Alicia." I toss her an air kiss and pray she will wake up tomorrow morning. At ninety-two, one never knows.

7

Wednesday, October 26

HALLOWEEN IS RIGHT AROUND the corner. Morning arrives before I know it. I have slept like a dead log—which reminds me that Pepper needs to go outside and do his thing. I sit up and yawn. The house is cold. Apparently, the electricity is still out. But I'll brave the day.

I tug on my housecoat and shove my size nine feet in my furry house slippers, then check on Alicia. She's not in the guest bedroom.

As I head through the den, the lights pop on overhead.

Thank God for little favors. At least, we'll have our coffee, or tea. I find my guest seated in the recliner, snug under an Afghan, fast asleep as I tiptoe into the kitchen and fill the coffeemaker with water then add grounds to the filter cup. Two minutes later, the brew's dripping.

My first task is to let Pepper out in the backyard to perform his bodily functions. Thank God, the rain has taken a breath, but clouds overhead signal not for long. I am seated at the breakfast table contemplating our excursion to Dickson yesterday while biding time until I can phone Butch and report what I've learned. What *we've* learned. Alicia is a part of whatever this is. I smile to myself.

We'll solve this crime together.

I hear Alicia stirring in the den as the recliner comes up.

"Dorothy?"

"Yes, dear, I'm in the breakfast room." I hear feet hobbling across the wood floors and wonder how I'll fare when I'm ninety-two—if I ever reach that milestone. She looks older today and bedraggled.

"Do you have tea?" she inquires.

I get up from the table. "I'll make you a cup, sit down." I motion to my chair, already pulled away from the table and ready for occupancy. "Honey or milk with your tea?" I inquire.

"Both, thank you." She quietly sits in my chair.

Moments later, we are both at the table drinking our beverages.

"I should go home and check on my cat," she says.

"Sure, I'll drive you. I want to make sure nothing has been disturbed," I say as I get up and take our cups to the kitchen sink.

"Give me ten to get dressed and gather my things."

"No problem, I'll let Pepper back inside after his peeing session."

She laughs. "I intend to get myself a big guard dog."

"You do that, considering recent events." I know she's thinking of the menacing prowler. And the fact Lorita was murdered. What could be inside or outside the cabin that interests a prowler?

Twenty minutes later, with Pepper locked in his crate, I park in front of Clyde's cabin. I will never think of the structure as anyone's but his, though Alicia legally owns and occupies it.

We go inside together and switch on lights. I walk one direction while she ventures in the opposite direction. We meet in the middle, reminding me of an old country love song. Only the lyrics don't apply.

Nevertheless, it's a frivolous thought.

"Did you notice anything out of place?" I ask Alicia.

"No, but I want to let Susan romp a bit."

"We should take a walk around the cabin," I suggest.

"What are you looking for, Dorothy?" She cradles Susan in her arms. The Persian purrs like she's hit payload.

"I don't know, just being thorough." We are investigating.

We discover a set of large footprints at the backdoor of the cabin. Alicia jiggles the door knob. "It's loose, someone tried to break in."

I pause to stare. "If someone wanted inside, a door wouldn't have stopped them. Or him." Maybe it's a her, I think of the Russian woman that posed as Clyde's granddaughter when Lorene came to the cabin.

We're back at the front of the cabin.

"Thanks for letting me stay overnight," Alicia says.

"No problem. If you want to come back tonight, feel free."

She smiles sweetly. "I never expected to experience such fine hospitality—but then southerners are known for their generosity."

"Yes, we are." I beam at the compliment.

We take a moment to hug each other.

"Well, I should go now. You should report your prowler."

"Good idea." Alicia shows me the burner phone I purchased for her yesterday before leaving Dickson. "I'll call if trouble knocks."

"You do that." We hugged again and I drive home.

It's a fine autumn day, the clouds dissipating. It's pretty cold with the humidity on the low side. But the sun is a golden ball in the sky, a reminder of God's marvelous grace in creating a beautiful earth.

I thank Jesus for my long life as I smell the wealth of the forest floor bathed in matted wet leaves. I adore the Tennessee countryside.

The landline rings as I let myself into the kitchen.

"Hello!" I grab the phone attached to the wall. I won't give up my old-fashioned belief that landlines are a lifeline if cell towers fail. I've already ordered a new gas-driven generator since I cannot count the times the electricity has crashed in this house. *Like last night.*

"Who is this?" I ask when no one responds.

"It's me, Dorothy."

"Lorene, how is Heather?"

"Oh, feeling a bit more optimistic now that I'm here to take care of her. That's what mamas are for. I told her not to worry about the cancer spreading, that God is good and hears our prayers."

I hear a sniffle and know Lorene is frightened for her daughter.

"You're a good Christian, Lorene."

"I was wondering—did you go to Dickson?"

"Yes, yesterday. Alicia went with me. We talked to one of Lorita's friends and learned she received a gift of tea from a Secret Pal." I added Secret Pal, because Tina did not know who sent the package.

"What does tea have to do with Lorita's death?"

"Maybe nothing," I reply. "Maybe everything. The peach tea could have been laced with a poison. Butch has probably heard from the coroner by now and knows the cause of Lorita's death."

"Do you think Detective Peters will tell you what the coroner found out?" Lorene asks. "We're not officially involved, you know."

"I know, but I have a bargain chip." I'm planning what to do as I talk to Lorene. "I'll tell him if he shares what the forensic report says, I'll tell him what I found out in Dickson yesterday."

"Clever!" Lorene chuckles. "Oh, I hear Heather. Keep in touch."

"I will. When will you be home?"

"I'm not sure. Probably not for at least two weeks," she replies.

"Okay." And I realize Alicia and I will need to solve the crime.

I let Pepper out of his crate to run around, take a hot shower, then dress for the day in a warm pantsuit. Green. I look good in that color with my hair highlighted in a shade of red. This conversation with Butch deserves my best face-to-face encounter.

I drive into town and park out front of the precinct. The cop on duty waves me past and I take the elevator up to the second floor.

Ellie's chair is empty. But luckily, Butch is at his desk.

"Hello, Dorothy." He waves me into his office.

"Hello, Lloyd." I'll be extra nice today in addressing him.

"What can I do for you, Mrs. Powell?"

Not Dorothy? He's in a mood. Must have had a fight with Ellie.

"I have information regarding Lorita's death," I tell him.

"Okay. You have my attention." He leans back in his swivel rocker, his hands threaded at the back of his head, his mustard-colored eyes sharp as a tack on me. Tell me." It's more of a demand.

"Certainly." I take a seat. "But first, you give me something."

He lunges forward, the chair up-righting as his feet pound the floor. "Dorothy Powers, you are in no position to bargain."

"If you say so." I start for the door. "See you later."

"Wait! What do you want?"

"To see the coroner's report—what killed Lorita," I reply.

"Why?"

"Because what I have to tell you may be pertinent."

"Okay." He settles down and removes a folder from his desk drawer. Seeing his cooperation, I return to my seat and read the report.

"I was right!" I exclaim. "Poison tea killed Lorita."

His bushy graying eyebrows lift, his wiggling lips in a twist. "You knew. How did you know?"

"Are you sure you have the time? An important detective like yourself," I tease then launch into my story of what happened when Alicia Colby and I took an excursion to Dickson, Tennessee yesterday.

8

Friday, October 28

IT IS A BLUSTERY AUTUMN morning with the wind kicking leaves all over my yard like a football game is in process. I am dressed and ready to leave for the Senior Citizen Center by eleven a.m. As I venture out to get in my car, I am nearly blown away, yet determined to win against the weather. Alicia is watching through her front window as I pull my BMW up in her yard in front of the cabin. She hurries out, checking the door to see that it is locked. Wearing a thick, water-proof parka that covers her head and reaches down to her knees, I note the thick leather boots she has on. I suspect England has its bad winters, too.

Like me, she's dressed to battle the blustery day.

"Good morning!" I hail as she scrambles into the passenger seat, sighing like she'd been beat to death by the terrific wind.

"Same to you." There is no smile.

I turn half way in my seat. "Are you sure you're up to coming with me today?" I do not want this to be the elderly woman's last excursion.

Her greenish-black eyes widen as if surprised by my question.

"I hope you're not thinking I'm too old to go out on a day like this." I suddenly see spunk in her that seems to surface like a storm.

"No, of course not." I back out of the driveway.

We ride down the gravel road that meets the main highway and I turn the car toward Columbia in silence. I wonder if Alicia has phoned Butch as I suggested and told him about her suspect prowler.

"I called Detective Peters," she suddenly reveals.

I chuckle. "Are you a mind reader? I was just thinking about the same thing." I slow down for a truck to pass us on the curvy highway. "Why are people always in a hurry to get somewhere?" I ponder aloud.

"He gave you the middle finger—did you see that?"

"No, thank God! I don't need anybody's curses today, with the weather this nasty. We may get some ice tonight," I said.

"Well, I'll be fine if the electricity doesn't crash."

"You'll be fine because you are staying the night with me again," I decide. "No, it's no imposition, and I have food in the freezer. Besides, my new generator works just fine. It was installed yesterday."

Alicia is super quiet.

"Do you have other plans?" I inquire.

"No, I was just thinking I might sell the cabin and move into town. Maybe an assisted-senior-citizen complex."

"Please give yourself a chance to acclimate," I say. "I really don't want to lose you as a neighbor. We'll figure out what happened to your great niece and make dadgum sure the perpetrator pays for his crime."

Assuring myself I am a competent detective by my God-given gifts of above-average intelligence and determination, I smile.

Alicia sighs. "I'll see how this winter goes."

By then, we are passing the City Limits sign. The Senior Citizens Center is located in a building in central Columbia. I circle the historic courthouse and find a parking space nearby since we are early for lunch. We get out of the car and walk to the entrance.

"Lorene Perkins usually comes with me." Alicia and I step inside the facility and inhale the delicious odor of baking chicken. "I learned last night her daughter Heather is having cancer surgery today."

"I hope all will go well." My neighbor is out of breath.

"Let me find a seat for you, then I need to greet a couple of my friends." I spy Elizabeth Hinson and Jane Murphy talking to the new manager of the Center. Lizzy is in my Sunday School class at First United Methodist. Jane is Presbyterian. They play canasta with me and Lorene every Friday afternoon between two and five p.m.

"I'll be fine," Alicia says. "Ask if I can have a hot cup of tea, I'm chilly." She shrugs off the heavy fleece-lined parka and laces her petite fingers on top of the speckled Formica table. "Go! Greet your friends!"

"I'll be back in a jiffy." I hang my coat on the back of a chair next to hers. "Hot tea, coming right up. Honey and cream, right?"

"Right." She smiles weakly, appearing a little shaky.

I mosey past Clint Howard, the new manager of the Senior Citizen Center. I heard he's a retired RN and has an apartment in town. He's younger than me, and has a full head of thick white hair. Arthur lost most of his in his mid-forties, but he refused to shave his head, so he always looked wind-blown with pink skin showing.

Lizzy is whispering to Jane and pointing.

"Hello, girls, am I interrupting something important?"

"Oh, hi, Dorothy," Lizzy says. "Who is the old gal with you?"

"My new neighbor," I reply. "Alicia Colby from England."

"Really?" Jane takes off her bifocals to view my guest.

"She's Clyde Willems' great aunt—he was murdered two years ago by the same hit man who took out my Arthur and Lorene's Crawford."

"I read about all that two years ago," Clint Howard remarks as he interrupts our conversation. "Another fellow was also murdered."

"I'm Dorothy Powell," I introduce myself.

"The school janitor, I believe," he recalls.

"Yes," I say, daring to look him in the eye. He is so young and handsome I am embarrassed to be blushing in his presence. I feel giddy, like a teenager with a crush. I avert my gaze quickly.

"Daniel Jackson was his name, I believe."

"Yes, right again." I force my eyes on him, "I'm helping his granddaughter Zoey with her college tuition," I proudly announce.

This is news to Lizzy and Jane. I don't tell them *everything*.

"I had no idea," Jane remarks. "You're a good woman."

"Yes, she is." Mr. Howard wickedly smiles at me.

I begin to melt like a Swiss cheese on hot toast.

"And a very classy and smart lady," he adds as if he knows me.

His comment makes my crush on him multiply exponentially. In the corner of my eye, I spy Alicia standing at the food counter.

"Excuse me, my friend asked me to get her a cup of hot tea."

Jane waves me off. "She can do that by herself. How old is Alicia?"

"Ninety-two, but she's quite capable of caring for herself." I wonder if that is true now that she's talking of moving into a senior-citizens complex. "I should pay her some attention."

"That old?" Lizzy frowns as I turn to walk away.

"Oh, Dorothy . . ." Mr. Howard snags my arm.

I freeze and turn around to face him. "Yes, Mr. Howard?"

"Clint, please." He grins.

"Clint," I mutter and wait to see why he's stopped me.

"We should get together over a cup of coffee, Dorothy. And talk sometimes. I have questions regarding your husband's death."

His oversized black-olive eyes are cast in long eyelashes.

"Why?" Lizzy notices us talking. "Are you writing a book?"

He looks down at Lizzy, half a foot taller than she.

"Just trying to get to know my clientele," he replies.

"What about it, Dorothy?"

"Sure," I nervously answer, questioning his motivation.

I take Alicia home after lunch and return to the Center for our regular Canasta card game. Phyllis Gatewood is filling in for Lorene.

We four sit at the table as Jane deals the cards. Phyllis is my Canasta partner. "So, have you heard from Lorene, how her daughter came through surgery?" she asks while studying her card hand.

"No, but she'll likely call tonight," I say, joyful I have three aces and a wild black two in my hand. Not to mention one red three. I will have the first opportunity to meld since I sit on Jane's left.

"I do pray Heather will be okay," Lizzy comments. "I had a niece that died from breast cancer. It's an awful disease."

We each draw a card and discard around the table. My turn comes so I lay down three aces, which adds up to more than fifty points.

Lizzy also melds with four wild cards. She's after a thousand points in this game, but I will do everything possible to defeat her team.

"I think Clint is sweet on you," Jane casually comments.

"No, he just wants to pick my brain," I dismiss her comment.

"No, he wants more than that!" Lizzy says. "I saw the way he looked at you, Dorothy. You have a fine figure."

I sit back. "You think he wants to have sex with me?"

They all chuckle.

"I won't go that far!" Jane says.

"I heard he has a girlfriend in Nashville," Phyllis reveals. "I think he's writing a novel about what happened to Arthur and Crawford."

"That makes more sense," Jane agrees.

"Dorothy is too old for him—what is it? Seventeen years?"

"Clint is only sixty-five?" My heart drops in my chest. I was hoping for late sixties. I knew women that married men seven years their junior. I could stretch the difference for a guy like Clint.

The game goes on for another fifteen minutes.

"I'm out." Jane lays down all her cards as she finishes out the wild-card suit of seven and closes two others. "Sorry, gals."

"You're not a bit sorry!" Phyllis frowns.

I lay down my one counting card in my hand. "You win this one."

We hear the wind roaring outdoors. Windows rattle. Around four we all decide to end our card game early and go home. I still need to fetch Alicia before the roads are too treacherous to negotiate.

It is dark by the time we are safely inside my house. I have a message from Claire on my cell phone. "Mama, we're in for an ice storm tonight, don't you dare go anywhere tomorrow until it melts."

Alicia chuckles. "She sounds like my mother."

"My Claire is so bossy I want to clobber her sometimes."

We both laugh. Then the electricity crashes. A few seconds later, I gratefully hear the sound of the Generac pumping out electricity.

"I'm glad you insisted I spend the night again with you," Alicia says. "You are the best friend I have ever had, Dorothy Powell."

"And you are a gift, Alicia Colby. Shall we heat us some supper?"

9

Saturday, October 29

LLOYD PETERS SPENT THE night at Ellie's apartment. They had been engaged for two years, but she'd refused to let him move in with her. The ring on her left fourth finger was symbolic he would marry her if he wanted to live under the same roof. As of late, she'd been withholding sex from him, stating their relationship would be more meaningful if they were celibate on their first wedding night.

She broke her rule last night.

"I'm mad at you," Ellie says to Butch as she crawls from bed. "You got me intoxicated and took advantage of me."

He sniffles. "Seems to me you were a willing partner."

Ellie frowns and throws a pillow in his face. "I hate you."

"No, you love me." He pulls her back into bed. "Do we have to wait until Christmas to get married?" He's sampled the product.

"My mother would kill me after all the planning she's done," Ellie reminds him. "She hated Richard." That was her first husband. "We eloped and she never got to dress up a church for her only daughter."

Lloyd frowns. "Okay, but do we have to give up sex for the next two months?" It's not his idea of mentoring a loving relationship.

"I suppose it's impossible for a guy to understand." She abandons the bed and goes into the bathroom, slamming the door.

He looks at the closed door. "So, we're not negotiating?"

The door opens. "No!"

He drops his head on the pillow. "Well, I don't like it."

They are dressed for the day and on their way to the office when Ellie says, "Are you going to warn Dorothy Powell?"

Lloyd rubs his chin as he cuts a corner with his vintage Chevrolet K-5 Blazer. "I haven't decided. Ignorance is bliss."

"Not if that scumbag decides to pay her a visit."

Ellie is talking about Mark Hagen, the hitman that killed four men from Maury County two years ago. Dorothy's husband Arthur was the first to die. His neighbor Crawford Perkins met his death the same day. Both found on Crystal Creek on their own properties. The Tennessee Bureau of Investigation was trying to determine how Hagen escaped a maximum-security prison located near Knoxville, Tennessee.

The case ramped up when Lorita Willems was found dead in her Dickson apartment. The local police were advised to keep that information close to the vest. Captain Marilyn Colbert agreed.

"I don't want to frighten half of the senior population in Columbia," Lloyd replies, pulling into a space in front of the precinct.

Ellie is out the passenger door without assistance. The wind is wicked today but the sky is a swath of blue overhead, and the sun is shining. She'll take a weather gift in October like this any day.

A few minutes later, Lloyd is unlocking the door to his second-floor office. Ellie goes in first and switches on lights. He walks over to her desk and retrieves a pack of written messages he failed to tend to yesterday, hoping some of the problems resolved themselves.

"Why didn't you tell me Captain Colbert called me yesterday?"

Ellie sits at her computer and turns it on. "You said you did not want to be disturbed." She glances up. "I obey the boss."

"Cute." He smirks as he slams the door to his office.

Ellie's new rules of engagement do not sit well with him. Withholding sex is no way to hook a fish on the end of a sharp lure.

The landline rings in Marilyn's office. Bessie answers.

"Can I help you?"

"Detective Peters here, is Captain Colbert available?"

He waits, dreading what lays ahead of him in the next few minutes. Nobody blows off Marilyn. She's a veteran officer that does not put up with unprofessional county employees. "Colbert here."

"It's Lloyd Peters," he says. "I apologize for not getting back to you yesterday." He waits for a lecture that does not come.

"You missed a meeting, Detective. Agent Gilbert Goode was here to meet with me about the ongoing investigation into Lorita Willem's recent death. I called you as a courtesy. But you were busy."

"Will you update me?" He didn't want to cast blame on Ellie.

"No. Privileged information," she replies.

Lloyd wants to slam down the phone and grab Ellie by the neck and choke the living daylights out of her for not alerting him to Colbert's call. "I'm truly sorry, Captain."

"I'm sure you are. You might bring Dorothy Powell into the equation—warn her to be on the lookout for the fugitive, Mark Hagen," Marilyn suggests. "He might want to get even with her."

"I'll take care of the matter." Lloyd does not want to irritate Colbert any more than he already has. "Good day, Captain."

He sits at his desk as the connection dies without a benediction.

"Well, that was certainly disappointing," he complains.

"What did she say?" Ellie stands in the doorway. "I'm sorry, Lloyd. I should have told you she phoned. But you weren't very nice to me yesterday." There are tears in her huge emerald eyes.

Lloyd gets up and walks over to Ellie and wraps his arms around her. "We've both got the wedding jitters, sweetheart. Why don't we just elope over Thanksgiving and forget about the big ceremony?"

Ellie pulls away and looks up at Lloyd. "I can't, sorry."

"And I apologize for being an insensitive jerk." Yesterday was a rotten day with too many legal issues to track. "I'll make it up tonight."

"Not in my bed," she says. "But you can treat me to a steak."

He kisses her. "Anything you say, sweetheart."

The messages are all answered and stowed away by lunchtime. Ellie is typing and does not notice when he leaves the office. He's phoned Dorothy Powell's landline but she is not answering, so he will drive out to her place and take a look around, to be on the safe side.

* * *

The Chevy Blazer is far too familiar as it crunches gravel in my driveway moving steadily toward my house. *Butch!* What does he want? I ponder. He pulls into the circular drive and kills the motor.

I walk over to the driver's side as his window comes down.

"Ms. Powell." He tips his hat.

"Nice day for a drive in the countryside, Detective. *May* I help you with something?" I make dadgum sure I use the right verb.

He crawls out of the vehicle and stretches his lithe body. Gym perfect, Ellie's been working him out in bed, it appears.

"Isn't it a bit cold to be raking leaves?" he notes the colored collection inside my two large garbage bins.

"Not for me." I'm dressed for the weather. "My yardman came down sick with influenza, and I absolutely despise a messy yard."

Lloyd pulls the collar to his coat closer around his neck. "Well, I'm cold. Can we go inside and talk a bit?"

Can you? I think to myself. He's already mounting my front porch, so I know the option to say no to his visit is null and void.

"Anything to make your day better, Butch." He hates my calling him that. "Why didn't you call first, I might have been busy?" I abandon my yard project and wonder what news he's brought me.

"Check your message center, Dorothy, I called."

"Oh." He's won this verbal round.

He trails me down the hall and into the breakfast room.

"Coffee?" I inquire.

"Sure."

He sits while I make fresh and place two mugs on the breakfast table, his black, mine doctored with cream and two sugars.

"What's brought you to my doorstep?" I get to the point.

He places his mug on the placemat, smoothing out the fabric. It's the same pattern Claire and I made two years ago, right after Arthur died. I'll never forget our mother-daughter sewing projects.

"A courtesy call," he replied. "I appreciate all you've done to help with solving Lorita's murder, but I think it's best if I work solo."

"Oh?" My lips pucker with distaste. "Why *now*?"

"For your own good, you don't need to be messing around in this nasty business," he proclaims. "Nosiness can be dangerous."

I sit back and take in his remark. "Are you here to warn me about something?" My blue gaze tightens on the savvy detective.

"I spoke with Captain Marilyn Colbert earlier today and she asks me to read you in on a problem," he says. "About Mark Hagen."

"That creep that killed my Arthur?"

"Yes, him."

"I don't see any reason to worry about a hitman behind federal bars, do you?" I find the coffee bitter and in need of more sugar.

It seems time stands still.

43

"What are you not saying?" I ask, leaning forward.

"Hagen recently broke out of prison."

"What?" Alarm chokes me. Could he be the prowler that left footprints on Alicia Colby's backdoor step? "When?"

"A month ago."

"Before Lorita Willems was murdered," I conclude.

"Yes." His hands fumble with a cigarette lighter.

"How did he escape a maximum federal prison?"

"I wasn't read in on the details," he replies.

"So, no one knows how he escaped," I conclude.

"Like I said, I wasn't read into the details."

I hear the rooster shoot out of my clock, registering two p.m. "Did you speak with Alicia Colby about her prowler?"

"No, that's my next stop. Is she at the cabin?"

I chuckle. "So, now I'm your secretary?"

Butch's face turns dark. "This is a courtesy call, Dorothy."

"I want to go with you to see Alicia," I decide. "The woman is frail and she feels safe with me. You're not so cozy around people."

"Whatever you say." He pushes back in the chair and gets up. "I don't have all day, so I'll pull up to the back door and get you."

"You do that."

I double-lock the front door after Butch and put on my short coat then secure Pepper in his crate, deciding not to take my purse.

10

ALICIA IS WEARING A HOUSECOAT as she opens the front door. It appears she has been weeping. "This is Detective Lloyd Peters," I introduce him. "He has some news he wants to share with you."

"Come in." Alicia widens the door and sniffles.

"Did you catch a cold, dear?" I inquire as Butch stomps his boots on the floormat. Wood crackles loudly in the fireplace.

"I caught a cold somewhere," Alicia replies and sneezes.

"We won't bother you long," Butch chimes in. "May we sit?"

Finally, he uses the correct English. *May we . . .?*

"Would you like a cup of tea?"

"No, thank you," Butch replies for both of us. "Dorothy just served coffee before we came over to visit."

I know *this* is more than a visit.

"Did Dorothy tell you about my prowler?" Alicia asks.

"Yes, but I'd like to hear from you about that," he replies.

"Well, it's happened several times during the night," she explains. "Once, Dorothy and I found a footprint at my backdoor."

"Did you snap a picture?" He removes a small writing tablet from his briefcase to jot down notes. "Show me." He walks through the living room into a small chamber that was once an open porch.

We follow Butch out the backdoor and stand there.

"There's no footprints here now," he notes.

"No, but I saw it. Made by at least a size thirteen shoe," I offer.

"Not my man." He ponders what I've told him.

"What do you mean, not my man?" Alicia asks.

"I sent someone out to walk your property every other night for the past ten days," he explains. "Tony wears a size nine shoe."

I'm aggravated at Butch. "Why didn't you tell Alicia?" I bark. "She's been so worried I've insisted she spend several nights with me."

He is incorrigible and I want to clobber him here and now.

"I didn't want to worry you, Miss Colby," he apologizes.

"Tell her everything!" I demand.

He points indoors. "Let's do this inside where it's warm."

We hover together in the living room as Butch repeats what he told me to Alicia, how a serial hitman escaped from prison. He doesn't wear a size 13 shoe, either, so Alicia's prowler must be somebody else.

"I once caught a glimpse of him as he fled into the woods," Alicia recalls. "He was big, a black man, I believe."

Dom, Lloyd thinks, but refrains from commenting. The Somalian owned the Starlight Lounge in Nashville when Zoey Jackson worked for Sonja Berioski. They fled the country to avoid arrest after it was proven they ran a prostitute ring. Were they back?

"What are you thinking, Detective Peters?" I ask.

"Nothing important," he lies.

"Do you think I'm in danger?" Alicia asks him.

"No, but it is curious why someone is hanging around the cabin," he admits. "Do you know the history of this cabin?"

Alicia sneezes and wipes the drip with a handkerchief.

"My grand-nephew's father purchased the cabin," she replies. "After his death, Clyde moved in. Been here decades. When he was murdered, Lorita inherited the property. She didn't want it."

"So, she gave it to you," Butch concludes.

"Yes, she contacted me a good two years ago and I accepted."

I note how Alicia is struggling with her cold. "Shall I make tea?"

"Thank you, Dorothy." She clasps her hands in her lap.

From the kitchen, I can still hear their conversation.

"Do you think Clyde left anything valuable in the cabin?"

"I don't know, Detective Peters. The walls have been stripped and redone, so I know for a fact there are no secret chambers."

I chuckle to myself as the water boils in the teapot. Alicia is accustomed to old castles with secret chambers, ghosts of the past.

The two of them are discussing Lorita's death. Alicia mentions the gift her grand-niece received prior to her death. "Dorothy and I talked with a friend of Lorita's, a woman who worked with her at Cracker Barrel. Tina told us about the gift. Did the police find the container?"

"Not that I know of," Butch answers.

I hand Alicia her cup of tea with cream and honey added.

"Was my niece poisoned?" Alicia asks him.

"Yes, forensic evidence proves it."

Our visit abruptly ends. We are on our way back to my house when I thank Butch for being truthful with Alicia.

"Do you think it's safe for her to stay in the cabin?"

"Tony will check on her every couple of nights until Mark Hagen is apprehended. Meanwhile, you be careful and lock your doors."

"I always lock my doors and I have a security system."

"Good. Hagen might decide to pay you a visit."

"That's a warm-and-fuzzy feeling," I quip. "I hope he enjoys looking into the barrel of Arthur's shotgun if he comes calling."

"Good ol' Second Amendment!" Butch laughs.

I wave at Butch as he drives away.

Poor Ellie Champ, she has her hands full with that boy.

After taking Pepper for a walk and I'm settled into the house with the doors securely locked, I phone Lorene in Kentucky.

"Hi, it's me. How is Heather doing after surgery?"

"She's in pain but the procedure went well. Dr. Quarrels removed her left breast and said he got all the cancer," she replies.

"That's good news! When are you coming home?"

"Not until she feels better."

I tell Lorene about our Canasta game on Friday and that Clint Howard flirted with me. She's surprised, and reminds me that I'm too old for Clint, and that he has an ulterior motive in flirting.

Then, I tell her what Butch told me, that Mark Hagen had escaped prison. "The coroner confirmed Lorita was poisoned. Alicia and I believe it was in the tea. But no container was found in her apartment."

"You need to be very careful, Dorothy."

"I will. Oh, I wish you were here, Lorene, I really miss you."

"Well, save some of the fun for me, please!"

"I certainly will."

To pass the evening, I load a vintage tape in the old VCR recorder and watch a flick starring Rock Hudson and Marilyn Monroe. As the story unfolds, I recall the time I went on a date with Arthur to see that same movie. Tears sting my eyes, so I shut off the recorder. While drowning in my loneliness and misery, my cell phone rings.

It must be Claire checking on me. I was wrong.

"Is something wrong, Clint?"

"No, Dorothy, I just wanted to say goodnight, and how much I enjoyed our visit today at lunch. Maybe I'll stop by your farm one day this week. You can show me around. Is that okay?"

"Are you looking to buy rural property?" I inquire.

"It has crossed my mind. I don't want to return to Nashville now that I've had a taste of country living and real southern hospitality."

"Did you grow up in Tennessee?"

"No, raised and bred in New York. But I think I've found a cozy southern spot here in Columbia to put down new roots," he says.

I ponder his invitation.

"About coming out . . ."

"Sure, call first," I decide. "What are you doing Halloween?"

"How about I come out around three and bring supper? You can show me around your farm. Later, we'll greet the Trick-or-Treaters."

"That sounds like a plan, Clint."

"Rest well tonight."

"You, too."

The landline is dead but I'm not. I've never had so much energy. I want to clean the house and buy flowers for every room. I think I might be falling in love. *Me?* What a silly ol' fool I've become!

11

Sunday, October 30

I AM AT SUNDAY SCHOOL fifteen minutes early. Elizabeth Hinson sits down beside me. "Did you have a pleasant Saturday?"

"Yes, the weather was wonderful, a little cold, but I raked leaves in my front yard," I reply. Lizzy is a gossip so I won't tell her about my visit from Detective Peters, or Mark Hagen's escape from prison.

"My daughter came over and helped me clean out the attic," Lizzy says. "I still have a lot of old furniture stowed up there."

"I'm grateful I took care of all that soon after Arthur died," I tell her. "My house is in good shape, so all I have to do is take care of myself." I see several other class members entering the room.

"Have you talked to Lorene? How is Heather?" Lizzy whispers.

"They got all of her cancer, but had to remove a breast."

"That's a shame, she's so young. Her husband won't like that."

I don't comment about sex. I know men obsess about women's breasts, but it's none of my business, or Lizzy's, what Jim thinks.

"Welcome, friends!" our Sunday School teacher says, signaling it's time to study the Bible and leave our worldly cares aside.

After church, I go out to Barks Seared Pork for lunch.

"Are you by yourself today, Dorothy?" Charlie Bark asks, grasping me by the elbow as he escorts me to a small table.

I'd heard that Charlie was recently divorced, so his intimate act bothers me a bit. He was in his late fifties and, surely, has no designs on me. But I wonder if my money makes a difference.

"Yes, I'm alone." I disconnect myself from his grasp.

"Well, Lucy Bell will be right over to take your order. Enjoy!"

"Dorothy!"

I look up, stunned. Clint Howard is standing there, tall and handsome, and practically sucking the breath out of me.

"Clint." I am reminded of Marsha, and I forget the guy's name, but their relationship was often the topic of fun eons ago.

"What a nice surprise to bump into you," he says.

"Yes." I look around to see if he's alone.

"May I join you?" he asks, then sits down before I answer.

"Sure." Is it just me? Or are men hitting on me? I'm eighty-two years old and think a romantic relationship is far too risky.

"Have you ordered yet?" he asks.

"No, Charlie just seated me. Are you with someone?"

"No, I'm alone like you."

Alone. I recall how I hated that word right after Arthur died at the hands of Mark Hagen. "Well, then, we'll have lunch together."

"Yes, we will." Lucy Bell arrives with our water glasses.

As Clint's huge black-olive eyes capture me, I feel self-conscious. I want to ask if his friendship is sincere, or is he just a big tease?

I don't ask, I just bask in my opportunity—that this fantastic-looking intelligent man is actually interested in spending time with me.

"I was going to call you tomorrow and ask if you wanted me to bring a couple of packages of pre-wrapped candies," he says.

When Clint snaps his paper napkin across his lap, the sudden sound startles me. I glare at him. "Candy for what?"

"Halloween. Did you forget I was coming over to your house and bringing supper?" He stares as if I'm having a senior moment.

"Oh, yes, Halloween." I am rethinking having him all alone with me in my house. He's too clever and I'm far too infatuated with him.

"What? I see that question on your face."

I open my mouth then rethink what to say.

"Go ahead, Dorothy, I'm a grown man and can take it."

"I'm concerned about our, uh, visit, Monday evening."

"About our date, you mean?"

He's clarified his intent and I'm terribly flattered, though quite uncomfortable with the idea. My face is flushed with embarrassment.

"There's not a woman somewhere?" I burst out before thinking.

"No, no, Dorothy." He reaches across the table and pats my hand. At his touch, I tingle all the way up my arm and down my spine.

"You know I'm much older that you are, Clint."

Let's be real here, shall we?

He sits back, appearing wounded. "When did we start counting the differences between our ages? Relationships are built on caring."

I adore everything he's saying, but am reminded of Lorene's warning to beware, that he wants something from me. *Sex? Money?*

Then I consider what having someone like Clint in my life would mean. Someone to share my thoughts and keep me company.

My bed again. I would not need to feel *alone*.

"Are you ready to order?" Lucy Bell restlessly looks at me. I never saw her approach. My gaze is glued to the hunk across from me.

"My treat, Dorothy. What do you recommend?"

He peers at me for an answer. *A quick frisk in the bed?*

Lucy Bell pipes, "The pork plate is our special today."

I nod, tongue-tied and flabbergasted to be sitting here with Clint Howard, plus he is buying my meal, plus I'm a decade plus older.

"Now, Dorothy. Tell me all about yourself," Clint says as Lucy Bell walks away with our menus and orders.

I lean forward and take a breath. "Are you FBI?"

He sits back, a smile tugging at his lips.

"Why do you think that?"

I feel like a spider under a microscope.

"My friends think you want something from me," I admit.

His lips fold into his mouth in thought. "Friendship?"

"They think you're writing a book," I declare.

"About what?"

"My Arthur, and how he died. Are you?"

"No."

"Are you lying to me?" I ask with unbelievable boldness.

"No, I'm not writing a book, and I'm not working for the FBI. I manage the Senior Citizen Center because I enjoy people. My wife died a long time ago and I'm not divorced. I'm a back-slidden Lutheran."

I think about what Clint said. "Okay."

"Okay?"

"Yes, Clint. I like you, but I don't want to be played for a fool. If you want to write a story about what happened in Columbia two years ago, I'm fine with that. I'll be happy to share." *There!*

"Wow, Dorothy! You're quite a woman!"

* * *

Ellie broke her vow to be celibate again Saturday night, right after a delicious steak dinner at the newest restaurant in Columbia. Lloyd was in bed with her at her apartment, just lying there and thinking he was such a lucky man to have found a beautiful smart woman like Ellie.

She rolls over in the bed and frowns.

"I want you to go home, Lloyd."

"Why, we could have a lazy Sunday together. I was thinking of spending another night." He winks. "We can pick up your car tomorrow morning." He fiddles with the buttons on Ellie's PJ's."

"Stop it!" She pushes his hands away. "Go home. *Now!*"

"Is this about breaking your vow last night?" he asks. "Because if it is, I forgive you. We can live happily-ever-after from now on."

Ellie leaps from the bed and faces her fiancé. "My mother would be so disappointed with me if she knew how weak I am."

Lloyd's lips wiggle. "You gonna call her and tell her you've been a naughty girl and slept with me? I expect she wouldn't be surprised."

Ellie throws a pillow in his face. "Please. Don't do this."

Lloyd hugs Ellie. "This, loving you with all my heart."

Ellie is torn between letting go and holding on.

"Honey, we're already married, one in God's sight. I've committed everything I am and own to you, don't you know that?"

She nods, tears in the corner of her lovely green eyes.

Lloyd gets up and pulls on his pants.

"All right, Ellie, I'm going now. We'll play this your way."

"You mean that?" Ellie relaxes, lays back on her pillow.

"Yes, we'll keep our relationship on a business level until after the wedding—which means I don't need to take you out to supper or buy you expensive wines. We'll just do our jobs together. Okay?"

Ellie frowns. "You always have a twist to things."

He laughs. "I take that as a compliment."

"Which reminds me, did you tell Dorothy Powell everything?"

"*Everything?* Some things are best left unsaid," he points out. "The truth would only propel her to do really stupid things."

"She will, anyhow." Ellie watches Lloyd button his shirt. "I'll take an Uber to the office tomorrow. Nine o'clock sharp! Don't be late."

He salutes her. "No warm and fuzzy kiss goodbye?"

"You've had all the warm and fuzzy you're getting, buddy." Ellie walks him to the door and gives him a shove. "Don't come back."

The door closes in his face. He listens through the keyhole.

"Are you sure, Ellie?"

"I am," she says, leaning against the door.

"See you tomorrow, sweetheart."

12

Monday, October 31

TWO YEARS AGO, THE weather had been cold with a snow front barreling down on Tennessee from the northwest. This afternoon, it is balmy and storm clouds collect overhead in bundles of charcoal threaded with blinking lightning. I stand on my front porch looking up at the sky and wonder why I didn't cancel my date with Clint. No parent is bringing their children to my doorstep for treats in terrible weather like this. There might even be a spin-off tornado.

I hear the phone ringing and run down the hall to my breakfast room and grab the receiver. "Hello!" I hail with a fleeting breath.

"It's me, Mama. I thought I'd drive over with my grandchildren and keep you company tonight. We can have a party inside."

"Doesn't your church have a special Halloween celebration for the children?" I ask, simply because I have not told Claire about Clint.

"They do, but I'd rather spend the evening with you. I'll bring sleeping bags and the kids can bed down in the den. We'll have a fun sleepover," Claire says. "We should be there within the hour."

"No, Claire," I say, "I'm having company."

The airways sizzle with lightning.

"On a night like this?"

"Yes, a friend is coming over for supper to keep me company," I explain. "Besides, it's too bad a night for you to drive all this way. I'm fine, really. We'll do it another night."

I don't like how Claire is not arguing with me.

"Mama, is this friend a male?"

I nearly croak at her question. "Does it matter?"

"No, I guess not. Who is the man?"

"The newest manager of the Senior Citizen Center," I reply. "We hit it off, so he's coming over for a visit. I think he's writing a book."

"About what?" she inquires.

"What happened here two years ago, Claire, when Arthur, Crawford Perkins, and Clyde Willems were murdered."

"It's not healthy for you to dwell on the past, Mama."

"I'm not. I won't." But she's probably right.

"I don't like you letting strangers inside your home when you're alone," Claire fusses, the over-protective daughter who worries about me. "What do you really know about this man?"

"I know he's pleasant." I don't tell her he's seventeen years younger than me. "And I enjoy his company. Isn't that enough?"

"I remember when you let that bad man in your house and he abducted you," Claire fusses. "I was terrified, Mama."

"Clint is not a serial killer," I tell her, and will absolutely not divulge that Mark Hagen escaped from a federal prison a month ago.

"Okay, but call me when he leaves, okay?"

I think about that promise and wonder if Clint will want to spend the night with me. Naughty thoughts slither through my mind.

"Okay, I'll call if the wind doesn't take down the towers," I qualify my response. "Oh, Claire, I will be just fine. Don't worry so." I think of all the times I worried about her when she was dating.

Is that what I'm doing? *Dating?*

"Okay, have a nice evening."

Claire ends the call as my front door bangs with the wind.

"O, Lordy!" I forgot to shut it when I heard the phone ring.

A dark shadow stands in the doorway. My heart drops in my chest, keeping double-time with my scattered thoughts.

"Who is it?" I think of a horror movie I once watched where a wolf-man came out on stormy nights and devoured young women.

But then, I'm not young.

The shadow becomes a human face. "Clint?"

"Yes, Dorothy, it's me. Your door was open, so I came on in."

"Please close it for me and turn the lock." I am relieved.

He walks down the hall toward me and the closer he gets the more chills ripple through me. "I thought about canceling," I admit.

"I hoped you wouldn't." He stands in front of me, a hand fondly on my shoulder. "But I didn't want you to be alone on this stormy Halloween night." He sheds his parka and glances around.

I look up at him. I'm tall. Five feet, ten inches. But Clint is at least six four. I feel dwarfed standing so close to him.

"You have a nice home. It's misting rain, so I suppose I'll have to see your farm another day." He hooks his arm in mine.

We walk together down the hall to my breakfast room.

"Are you hungry?" he asks. It's already four fifteen, but feels much later. "I've had a busy day, Dorothy. Let's eat something."

I am mesmerized by his green eyes, dark and mysterious against his perfectly tanned complexion. "What's in your sack?"

"Kentucky Fried Chicken, biscuits, mashed potatoes, and green beans," he replies as he places the food on the table.

"Have a seat at the table," I say.

"Do you want ice tea or coffee?"

"Tea sounds refreshing, I'll fix it."

Without my instruction, he gathers two glasses from the cabinet and fills them with ice cubes from the freezer portion of the fridge.

"The tea is in a jug in the fridge," I say, loving he's made himself at home. I think he'd fit just fine in my kitchen. And elsewhere . . .

"Got it."

And he has, to perfection. How can this wonderful thing be happening to an elderly woman like myself? Am I dreaming? Or does Clint really care about me? I can't think about that. Time will tell.

We dine on paper plates and discard what remains. I suggest watching a movie, but Clint wants to talk. "Tell me what happened two years ago to your husband," he says. "How you felt about it."

He sits comfortably in Arthur's recliner, which fits him well.

"Be honest with me, Clint. Are you really writing a book?"

"I admit your lift story is quite intriguing, but even more, *you* interest me." He studies me. "Everything about you interests me."

"Okay." I begin with the time I first learned of Arthur's death when Clyde Willems came to my front door and told me. How Butch—Detective Lloyd Peters—suspected me of murdering him for the insurance money, and the fact I didn't know he took out a policy.

I must have talked forty-five minutes without stopping when the electricity crashed around six. "Don't worry, I have a generator."

Just like magic, it performed its duty.

"I don't think you will have guests tonight," Clint says. "Maybe I should go before the roads get swamped with water and dicey."

"You can stay longer if you want."

"Thank you, but no. It's been a pleasant evening, Dorothy."

"For me, too." I hear the wind kick up a notch outdoors. "Maybe it's safer for you stay here till this nasty storm moves through."

The windows shake as a tree loudly crashes to the ground in my backyard. Before I know it, Clint has me by the arm and asks where the closest bathroom is located. Together, we hug in my shower as the wind collapses my roof. I realize we are in the path of a tornado.

"Oh, Clint!" Has this new happiness brought me disaster?

He hugs me tighter. "It's okay, Dorothy, you're safe with me."

Fifteen minutes later, when we exit the bathroom, I see the trunk of a large oak with scratchy branches stretched across my den.

"What a huge mess!" Pictures have fallen off the walls and water has pooled all over my wood floors. My furniture soaked, ruined.

The place is uninhabitable so I start to bawl.

"You can't stay here tonight," Clint says. "Come home with me."

What will Claire think? I hesitate to answer him.

"It's your best option." He waits for my approval.

"Okay, let me get my purse in the bedroom."

"Stay put, I'll get it, the roof is unstable."

I wait for him, shivering in the chilly night air. The tornado has sucked all the humidity out of the air. I wonder what it's going to cost me to repair or replace everything. I'm suddenly depressed.

"I should call my daughter and tell her."

"Later, it's not safe in here." He's already dragging me through the den toward the breakfast room, down the hall, and out the front door. His car lies under a bushy branch, so we take my BMW to town.

It's too dark and rainy to see how Columbia faired during the storm. He drives us straight to his apartment and shades me with his large umbrella as we enter the building. He lives on the second floor.

"I have a guest bedroom where you can sleep," he says.

I know he knows I'm concerned over how this looks. "I really need to phone my daughter Claire and tell her what's happened."

"Sure, but I'm betting the cell towers are down."

I look for a signal and find none. "You're right."

"Okay, let's go up and change out of our wet clothes."

I have no other option but to spend the night with Clint.

Not that I will sleep in his bed. And, to my chagrin, I didn't have time to pack an overnight bag. We walk up a flight of stairs to his second-story apartment and he lets us in with a key.

I am overwhelmed with indecision. *Stay or go.*

Clint is super neat and the living room looks clean and smells fresh. I sit quietly on his beige sofa, shivering, while he changes clothes in his bedroom. I feel guilty in not finding a way to contact Claire. She will hear about the tornado on TV and worry about me.

But, if I tell her I'm spending the night with Clint, she won't like it. She will get in her car and come and get me. *Not tonight.*

13

Tuesday, November 1

COLUMBIA IS IN SHAMBLES. Four tornados ripped through southern Tennessee taking out power lines and collapsing buildings. Debris is strewn everywhere, on rooftops, roads, and in trees. A doll hung in the crook of a bush and I wondered if the little girl was injured.

An F-3 demolished the whole block of Second Street. Butch's office building was untouched but the structure across the street lay in shambles. Good thing the storm hit at night, otherwise many people downtown working in business locations would have perished.

As Clint drives my car through town, he pauses to take pictures with his phone. "Channel 5 in Nashville will want these shots," he tells me. "We need to see if the historic courthouse is still standing."

"What am I going to do, Clint?" I ask.

"About your house? I'm sure you have adequate insurance."

"I do. I suppose I could stay with Lorene while it's being fixed." I suddenly think of Alicia. "I need to check on a friend."

"Okay, viewing the courthouse can wait, where does she live?"

"Behind my house, in Clyde Willems old cabin."

"Alicia Colby," he recalls. "I met her last Friday when she came to lunch with you at the Center." He refers to the Senior Citizen Center. "I'll check on the facility later to see if it's been damaged."

It's a messy drive through the countryside, but Clint is an excellent driver. He takes his time and avoids cars parked alongside of the road, probably abandoned during the terrible storms. "Hurry, please."

I worry a Tennessee storm has killed Alicia before poison tea has a chance. We pass by Lorene's farm and I miss her. By now, she's heard about all the damage. I know she'll come home soon.

"Look!" I point to my daughter's Buick parked in the driveway. "Claire must be beside herself!" I realize I never called her.

"She doesn't look too happy," Clint comments as he parks my BMW next to Claire's. I see her tears turn to pure anger.

"Uh oh, I'm going to get a verbal whipping from my daughter."

I get out of the car and wait for a lecture.

"Mama! I thought you'd been injured in the storm. I've called every hospital within fifty miles. Why didn't you phone me?"

I hug Claire and take a huge breath. "This is Clint Howard," I introduce my friend. "He was here when the tornado struck."

"Hello, Clint." Claire shakes his hand, but her gaze is on me. "Where did you stay last night?" Now, she looks at Clint.

"With me, in my guestroom," he qualifies and saves my butt.

"I was so upset, and the phone lines were down," I explain to Claire. "I'm so sorry, I was going to phone you this morning."

"But you haven't." She glares at Clint.

"Mrs. Burkes, I apologize for the mix-up, but we barely escaped getting killed last night," he tells Claire. "There were no hotels operating—you should see downtown Columbia."

A deafening silence follows.

"Okay, Mama . . ." Claire takes my arm and walks ten paces.

"He's not my boyfriend," I whisper in her ear. "I didn't sleep with him." I lock eyes with my daughter. "Honest, cross my heart."

Claire visibly wilts. "I didn't think that at all, I was just worried."

"I know, dear." I glare at my damaged house. "Do you think it's fixable? Or should I just take the insurance and move somewhere?"

Claire is surprised at my comment.

"It's up to you, but I'd love for you to move into a senior-citizen complex in Nashville closer to me," Claire says. "We'll get an insurance adjuster out here as soon as possible to assess the damage."

I walk back over to Clint. "Maybe you should leave," I say. "Has your car been damaged?" He drives a blue Ford Taurus.

"While you were speaking with Claire, I checked and it's running. A bush broke the windshield, but that can be fixed."

"If it's not safe to drive, I'll take you back to town."

"No, Dorothy. Spend some time with your daughter," he says, "I have plenty to keep me busy at the Senior Citizens Center."

"I hope the Center was not damaged," I say.

"Me, too, but lives are far more important than architecture."

He walks away and I somehow feel abandoned. Clint is a great guy, but I wonder how he knew Claire's last name was Burkes. I'm sure I never told him. It's a puzzle I will ponder on. *Alicia!*

I chase down Claire. "I need to see if my new neighbor is okay."

"I'll drive you, Mama." We get inside her Buick.

Claire maneuvers the gravel road laden with limbs. The land is torn up from the storm. As we approach from a distance, it appears the tornado skipped over Clyde's cabin. *Alicia's, now,* I need to start thinking. An idea pops. Maybe, I can stay tonight with her.

Alicia is standing in the yard as we pull up to the cabin.

"Oh, Dorothy! I have never been so frightened in my life!" she exclaims. "I spied the black cloud filled with lighting coming this way." She pointed toward my house. "Is everything okay?"

"No, it isn't." I say while hugging my friend.

"Who is this pretty lady?"

"Claire, my daughter." I remind Alicia that they've met before.

"Of course, Claire," she softly says then looks at me. "What happened to your house, Dorothy?"

"A large oak tree crashed through my roof and parked itself in my den," I reply. "I can't live in my house until the roof and interior damage have been repaired or replaced. I am homeless."

"Oh, dear. Do you want to stay with me?"

"It did enter my mind on the way over."

"Mama, you can come home with me," Claire intervenes.

I turn to look at her. "I know, but Alicia lives closer." My cell phone rings. "It looks like the phone towers are operating again."

"Hello," I say.

"Dorothy, it's Lorene."

"Oh, Lorene! I'm so glad you're in Kentucky with Heather, you missed the terrible storm that ripped through here last night."

"I'm home now. Sam called and said the tornado destroyed my barn," she explains. Sam is Lorene's son. He's a firefighter.

"Is your house damaged?" I ask, my worried gaze on Claire.

"I'll have a roofer check for missing shingles," Lorene replies. "I called to tell you I've had a visitor while I was away."

"What do you mean, Lorene?"

"I'll show you. Can you come over now?"

"Sure, but give me thirty. Claire and I are visiting with Alicia Colby. She's fine, the tornado skipped over her property."

"Thank God, tell her hello for me. Come as soon as you can."

"I will." I end the call. "Lorene has had a visitor."

"What does that mean, Mama?"

"I have no idea." I place my eyes on Alicia. "Will you be okay here alone for a while? I need to pack a bag, if I can get inside my bedroom. And then go over and see Lorene. I'll be back later today."

I cannot give her a time because everything is up in the air.

"Sure. You take care of business," Alicia says in her British accent. "I am so pleased to have company for the evening."

We make sure Alicia is safely inside the cabin before leaving.

"Did Lorene have storm damage?" Claire asks as she drives.

"Her barn was blown away, but no house damage."

"Great! She's a lucky homeowner." Claire drives off the road to avoid a large tree trunk lying across the gravel road. "I don't know if it's safe for you to go inside the house." She glances over at me.

"I need my makeup and toiletries," I say. "And a change of clothes. I have to go inside before the insurance cordons off the house and declares it unlivable." I can't imagine the day getting worse.

But it will, I'm soon to learn.

14

LORENE IS STANDING ON her front porch appearing forlorn and I wonder why as Claire parks her Buick in the curved front driveway.

"Maybe you should wait in the car while I talk to her," I say.

"Whatever you think is best, Mama."

I love that Claire trusts my judgment in this matter. I've shared what Lorene told me over the phone, about her uninvited visitor.

However, I have yet to learn whom she is talking about.

Without comment, I get out of the car and walk up to the porch steps where Lorene appears to be akin to the leaning Tower of Pisa.

"I'm so glad you're back." I give her a hug. "And I'm so sorry about your barn. Did any of your animals die?" I wait for clarity.

"My milk cow didn't make it." Lorene withers in front of me.

"You can buy another cow; I'm glad you weren't home."

"Me, too." She seems unmovable.

"What did you mean about a visitor?" I inquire.

"Better I show you." She abruptly turns and walks into the house. I wave at Claire then follow her inside, baffled by the secrecy. She is already out of sight, so I call out her name. "Lorene!"

"In here, Dorothy!"

I find her at the foot of the stairs leading to the second story. She goes up and I follow. She pauses at the door of her guest bedroom. "There!" She points to something inside the room.

I hurry down the hall and into the bedroom. I spy an unmade bed and a paper tray with leftover pizza sitting on the bedside table.

"So, one of your boys has been staying here?"

She shakes her head, then retraces her steps down the hall, down the stairs, and into the den. "And there!" She points to a recliner.

"I don't understand, Lorene," I admit.

"Someone broke into my house and has been sleeping in my bed," she almost moans the words. "Someone has been sitting in Crawford's recliner. Their shoes are parked next to it."

I see the pair of boots for the first time.

"You almost sound like the little girl in the children's story: 'The Three Bears,'" I tease her, then see the worry flooding her face.

"Who do you think would do this?" she asks.

I think of Mark Hagen, suddenly weak in my knees. I grasp the arm of a chair and find my way to the sofa without falling.

"Should I call the police and report the break-in?"

"I'm surprised you haven't already."

"I wanted you to see for yourself and advise me, Dorothy."

"I am no expert witness," I say, "but I can tell you that Alicia Colby has had night prowlers, one of whom was a policeman."

I should tell Lorene that the hitman broke out of prison.

"Is there something I should know, Dorothy?"

"Yes. Butch told me last week that Mark Hagen escaped from prison a month ago. He may have killed Lorita Willems."

"You think that killer is stalking us?" Lorene exclaims.

"Whoever it is wants us to know he can do anything he pleases."

"Why do you think that?"

"People are looking for something. What if Clyde Willems hid an important document that would incriminate the Mafia he worked for?"

"Does Butch think that, too?" Lorene is calming some.

"I don't know what he thinks. He carries his investigations close to the vest." I recall something a detective voiced in a movie.

"Maybe we should go talk to him about your theory."

"It's a hunch, but I have no proof, Lorene."

"Well, I'm going to report a theft as soon as you leave," Lorene decides. "Will you come back and spend the night with me?"

"I'm sorry, I already promised Alicia I'd stay with her."

"Oh."

"After the police write their report, call Sam and have him pick you up," I suggest. "I don't think it's safe for you to stay here by yourself. Whoever your visitor was, he might need his boots."

We giggle at my comment. I grasp my friend's hand. "It will all work out for the best, Lorene. God is good and takes care of us."

"I know He does, but it helps for flesh-and-blood to assist, too."

I smile. "I won't tell our pastor you said that."

We take a moment to glare at one another.

"Well, Claire is waiting in the car, so I should go now. Call me after you get settled in at Sam's place," I request. "I'll pray for you."

"Wait. How much damage did the storm do to your house?"

"A lot," I reply. "I might sell and move."

"Where?"

"Nashville, maybe. Claire wants me living closer to her," I reply. "I'm not getting any younger, Lorene. I often need her help."

I dislike the idea of interrupting my budding friendship with Clint Howard—which reminds me: how does he know Claire's last name?

I tell Lorene goodbye and walk to Claire's Buick.

"Is she okay?" Claire inquires as she starts the motor.

"She will be." I don't want to mention a squatter.

Over the airways, a Christian music station is softly broadcasting. One of Amy Grant's old tunes, I recall.

"Where to, Mama?"

"Columbia. I want to see if I can rent an apartment for a couple of months—until my house is repaired and I can either move in, or put it on the market for sale. I realize moving has become a reality.

Claire drives too fast, but I keep my mouth shut. Two miles down the road, she cuts off the radio. "Who is Clint to you, Mama?"

"A new friend, very nice, and I enjoy his company."

"What does he want?"

I'm taken back by her question. "Are you that big of a cynic? He runs the Senior Citizen Center, and I'm sure he's friends with all the elderly who frequent the establishment," I reply. "We're friends."

"Okay, if you say so." She stares at the road spooling under the car as we drive way too fast toward Columbia.

"You think I'm an old fool and in love, don't you?"

"Those are your words, Mama, but you should guard your heart," she warns. "He's too young for you, and I don't trust him."

"Whatever you say . . ." I am finished defending myself where Clint is concerned. I will take whatever time he will give me.

15

I AM DOG-TIRED BY the time Claire drops me off at my house. Ted has phoned and she needs to go home. "Thank you, dear," I say, "I'll let you know what the insurance adjuster says about my damage."

"I doubt that will be tomorrow," she comments with the Buick's window rolled down on the driver's side. "Don't go back inside."

I hold up my overnight bag. "I won't, since you've collected my things for me." I will spend the night with Alicia, and the hour grows late. Claire and I talked to every rental agent in town. No rentals available since so many people suffered storm damage in the area.

"Promise you will call me in the morning," she says.

"No boogeyman's going to get me and Alicia tonight," I say with determination. Arthur's shotgun is in the backseat of my BMW.

"Just don't do anything foolish, okay?"

Her motor hums, and I know she needs to leave. I can tell she is worried about me, probably more about my friendship with Clint, the mystery man. "Oh, Claire! Did you tell Clint your last name?"

"No, is that important?"

I throw a hand. "Go home to Ted, I'll be fine."

"Okay, Mama."

She backs out of the gravel drive and spins the Buick around to face the main road. I stand there watching her leave, wondering how Clint found out Claire's last name. Something's not quite right.

As I place my overnight bag in the passenger seat, I think of calling Clint and point-blank asking him how he knew. He said he wasn't FBI, or writing a book, so what is he doing wooing me?

It is a dark, moonless night. My car lights shine a cone on the gravel road leading to the cabin. Somehow, I feel relieved when I park in front of the cabin and see lights turned on in Alicia's living room. Smoke curls up the chimney. The air is chilly tonight, in the fifties.

I get out of the car, set my overnight bag on the ground, gather my purse and Arthur's shotgun, before locking up. The front door comes open and I see Alicia standing there. "Need some assistance?"

"No, thanks, but I'll need to make two trips." I stare at her.

"Hand me the gun, you can carry the rest." She glances warily around the yard. "And hurry up, please. I have news."

News? I can't imagine what could upstage a tornado.

As soon as I am inside, Alicia locks the door and leans against it.

"You should read this." She hands me a folded note.

I set down my purse and suitcase and take the note, carefully unfolding it in case it is evidence with criminal implications.

LEAVE OR BE BURIED IN THE CABIN.

I fold the note and hand it back to Alicia. "This is a theat."

She nods.

"We have to call Detective Peters and tell him about the note."

She nods again, then totters over to the sofa, collapsing.

"Have you called already?" I inquire, worried someone is outside the cabin watching us. What about hidden cameras? I am totally freaked over the threat. "Never mind, we're not staying here tonight."

She nods.

I approach her. "Pack a bag, we're going to Lorene's."

I see tears trickling down Alicia's cheeks. She's too old to experience this kind of trauma. I think of Mark Hagen. He must be behind everything that is going on the shadows of Maury County. It doesn't take more than five minutes for Alicia to pack a bag.

I scatter the wood in the fireplace so it will cool, then cut off all the lights inside the cabin except for one in Alicia's bedroom. Better a prowler thinks someone is home. "Are you ready to go?" I ask her.

She nods.

It is close to ten p.m. when I switch off the car motor in front of Lorene's two-story house. The porch lights pop on, and I see my friend as she comes out on the porch. "Back so soon?"

I roll down the window. "Can Alicia and I spend the night with you?" I'm reminded of Joseph and Mary's story in the Bible.

There is no room in the inn.

"Of course, come inside, it's cold out here," Lorene calls back.

We are inside the house and barely seated in the den when Lorene queries Alicia, "Is there something wrong with the cabin?"

"Yes." She hands Lorene the threatening note.

I watch as Lorene's lime-colored eyes grow huge, the note in her hand trembling as she hands it back to Alicia. "What does it mean?"

"It means I need to move out of the cabin," Alicia replies.

"Not so fast!" I gabber. "No sick bastard is going to chase you out of your inheritance, Alicia. Over my dead body, if they do!"

Startled, Lorene pipes, "And mine, too!"

By this time, Alicia is weeping. First Clyde dies, then his half-sister Lorita is murdered. And now someone has threatened to kill her if she doesn't move out of the cabin. We have to do something quick.

"I'm going to phone Clint," I decide.

"Why him?" Lorene locks her gaze on me.

"Well, since you left for Kentucky, we've kind of been dating," I reveal. "Just as friends, he says, but I really am a sucker over a good-looking younger man." I feel stupid for my unedited confession.

Yet, it is cleansing to bear the truth.

Lorene takes a moment to soak in my statement. "Do you think Clint is working for the police department?" She glances at Alicia.

"If so, he's undercover," I decide. "He knew Claire's last name, and I didn't tell him, nor did Claire. He's up to something."

"Okay, call Clint and tell him about my note," Alicia says.

I walk into the kitchen and phone his cell number. He immediately picks up. "Are you okay, Dorothy?"

"I'm fine, Clint. When I got to Alicia's cabin tonight, she showed me a note that was tacked to her backdoor," I reveal. "It said 'Leave or be buried in the cabin.' She's freaked out over the threat."

"Have you spoken to Detective Peters about the note?"

"No, Clint, I wanted your opinion. What should Alicia do?"

"She should take the threat seriously."

"I agree. We're spending the night with Lorene Perkins. It's too late to call Detective Peters, so we'll go down to the station and file a complaint in the morning," I decide. "I hope I did not wake you."

"No, and I'm glad you phoned. I'll see you tomorrow."

"You will?" My toes tingle with anticipation.

"I took it on myself to contact your insurance adjustor. I'm meeting him at your house tomorrow morning at eleven a.m."

"That was quick," I say. "You seem to know a lot of people." I want to ask how he knew Claire's last name, but I don't want to rock the boat, meaning if he's interested in me, I need to trust him.

"Goodnight, Dorothy. Be sure the security system is on."

"Lorene doesn't have one, but I have a shotgun."

He chuckles. "Just as good. Shoot any intruder!"

"I certainly will." Secretly, hoping it's Mark Hagen coming through a window in Lorene's house. I owe him big time.

Ending my call, I go back into the den to report what Clint said. Lorene and Alicia appear to be seated on pincushions by the look on their faces. "What did your friend say?" they simultaneously ask.

"Take the threat seriously and don't go back to the cabin."

Alicia folds and weeps.

"I know, honey, it's hard," I try to comfort her. "I'm homeless, too. We'll get through all this trauma somehow."

"As long as my house stands, neither of you are homeless," Lorene says as she paces the den. "I'll get your beds ready."

Alicia reaches out a bony hand and grabs Lorene by her nightgown. "Oh, thank you! Thank you, Lorene! Thank you."

I feel the same way, all mushy over friendships. There are all kinds in this world. God's friendship that is eternal as His Holy Spirit guides His sheep through a dark and troubled world. Human friendships that form because of proximity and shared ideas. And romantic friendships—like how I felt about Arthur, and how I am beginning to feel about Clint Howard. God is just so special a friend.

"We should try to get some sleep." I help Alicia mount the stairs to the second floor. Tucking her in bed feels right.

"I never expected to experience such grand hospitality," Alicia whispers as her eyelids droop. "I love you, Dorothy Powell."

"I love you, too, Alicia. Sweet dreams."

I tiptoe out of the bedroom and partially close the door. Lorene is standing there, listening. "She's a sweetheart."

"Yes, she is."

"I changed the sheets in the bedroom where my mystery man slept," she tells me. "But his smell lingers."

"It must be rotten," I declare and we both laugh.

16

Wednesday, November 2

DETECTIVE PETERS IS WORKING at his desk when I burst through the door unannounced. Ellie is not at her desk and my visit is urgent.

"What is it now, Mrs. Powell?"

He doesn't call me Dorothy, so I know I've upset him.

"Alicia Colby and Lorene Perkins are here, too," I announce. "Alicia received this threatening note last night." I approach and hand it to him. He stands up and walks over to the open door, not yet unfolding the paper. I wait patiently for him to read it.

"Would you like to come inside my office, ladies, or would you rather eavesdrop?" he hurls a question at them.

I despise that nasty man, but he's the best game in town.

"They'll wait outside," I tell Butch.

He turns around and walks back to his desk, sits down, and unfolds the note, his mustard eyes scanning the page.

He looks up at me. "Where was it found?"

"Tacked to Alicia's backdoor," I reply. "And you should know that an intruder has been staying in Lorene's house."

He scowls, "Why am I just hearing about this now?"

"Because Lorene just came home yesterday morning—to check on her house for storm damage—her barn was blown away."

He sits back in his swivel rocker, his eyes locked on me, his lips twisted to one side, a hand swinging his ponytail over one shoulder.

"What are you going to do?" I inquire

"I'll send a forensic team out to Lorene's house to see if her intruder left fingerprints. And, also Miss Colby's," he adds. "You ladies find a place to hang out until they have completed their work."

"Okay, will you call me when the team has finished?"

"I have your cell number." He glares at me.

"Thank you." I walk out of the office. "Let's go, girls?"

"Where to?" Lorene asks with Alicia glued to her side.

"Back to my house," I reply. "Clint is meeting an insurance adjuster there at ten thirty, then we need to find a place to hang out."

The elevator doors are parting as I give instructions.

"Then what?" Alicia asks.

"We do something to fill our time until the forensic team has finished with their investigation," I explain. "Butch's orders."

"Where will we go?" Lorene asks. "Oh, we could hang out at my son Sam's apartment," she suggests. "But it's pretty small."

"After we go to my house, I'd like a strong cup of coffee then we can decide where to have lunch. Butch will build a fire under the M.E."

"Goldie Locks. . ." Lorene chuckles, "Dr. Cynthia Preston."

"You know the medical examiner personally?" Alicia is surprised.

"My oldest son is dating her," Lorene replies.

"I presume she has bottle-blond hair," I interject.

"No, it's natural and she's beautiful. Totally an intellectual."

"Okay, enough about Cynthia," I say as the elevator doors swish open and we walk through the foyer and exit through the front.

"So, what is the plan?" Alicia asks.

"To live and let live," I quip. I know the best made plans don't always work out. I pause to take in a breath of fresh autumn air. It's a pleasant day outdoors. One would never guess a series of tornadoes blew through southern Tennessee's countryside on Monday night.

The drive seems brief as we contemplate our day. As I pull into my driveway, I spy Clint's blue Ford parked behind a white van out front. He's talking with Guy Rider, the All-State Insurance adjuster.

I shut off the motor and we all get out

"Ms. Powell, sorry you have so much damage," Guy tells me.

"Have you already been inside?" I stare at my messy yard.

"Yes, ma'am. We've taken interior pictures and checked the roof."

"Good. Oh, this is my new neighbor, Alicia Colby," I introduce her to Guy. "You know Lorene Perkins." He tips his hat to the ladies.

"Guy was early." Clint approaches, leaning loosely to hug me.

If he keeps doing that again, I'll melt like butter in his arms. *It's just a friendly hug*, I tell myself, and pray I am wrong. *He's trouble.*

"Any ballpark idea how much it's going to cost for repairs?"

"I'll work up the figures at my office and give you a call next week," Guy replies. "Meanwhile, don't go back inside, it's not safe."

"So, I've been told." I lock eyes with Clint.

"Well, my work is finished here." Guy drives away.

"What are you girls doing today while you're homeless?"

Lorene chuckles at Clint's comment.

"I take it that my statement has a reference," he says.

"Yes, I said the same thing last night to Lorene."

"And I said she'd never be homeless as long as I had a roof over my head," Lorene paraphrases. "We're going to town for coffee."

"Mind if I join you gals, my treat?"

I blush despite I am too old for anything to affect me in that way. But Clint does a number on my emotions. I have to find out what he really wants from me. Or I will be hopelessly in love and he will surely break my heart. "We'll meet you at Coffee Call," I decide.

We are riding in my BMW and passing the City Limit sign in Columbia before Lorene comments, "He really likes you, Dorothy."

I cast a quick look at my passenger. "We're just friends."

"I don't think so," Alicia chimes from the backseat, "I saw the way that young man looked at you, Dorothy."

"Young man, that's what I must keep reminding myself. Did you know he's only sixty-five? That's a seventeen-year-gap between our ages. No, girls, we are simply friends!" I pound the steering wheel.

"Since you lost twenty pounds and dyed your hair, you look ten years younger," Lorene tells me. "Get a face-lift and go for it!"

"What does, 'go for it' mean?" Alicia inquires.

"Romance. A man in your life. Adventure!" Lorene yelps.

"I'm old, girls, but I'm not a fool. Clint is hanging around me for a purpose. I just haven't discovered what game he's playing."

"That's a pretty sinister outlook on romance," Lorene pipes.

"If Clint truly is interested in dating me, he'll level with me. Don't you think it's strange he showed up in town soon after Mark Hagan escaped from prison? He says he's not FBI or writing a book, but what if he something more?" I speculate the outcome of our friendship.

"What else is there?" Lorene asks, then grabs her mouth.

"Exactly!" I comment. The CIA comes to mind.

17

MY CELL PHONE DINGS as Alicia, Lorene, Clint and I are seated at a table in Coffee Call. I hurriedly swipe the face of my phone. His lips wiggle in a smile as he sits across from me. That devil, I could kiss him to death! "Hello?" I avert my eyes as I answer my call.

"Ms. Powell, this is Lloyd Peters. Dr. Preston found your terrier running down the gravel road as she approached your house."

"You found Pepper! Thank God!" I exclaim.

Cynthia Preston is the new coroner for Maury County.

"Is my dog with Dr. Preston?" I inquire.

"No, he's with Ellie at her apartment. The little guy was pretty banged up from the storm," Butch explains. "She took him to the vet." He falls silent. "Want me to email you the bill?"

"Sure," I reply. "I can't pick him up right now."

"That's okay. I think Ellie is getting pretty attached to him."

"Email me her cell number and I'll arrange a time to pick him up." I realize I have no safe shelter for him or me.

"No worry, Ellie is fine keeping him for a while," he says.

The call falls dead and I realize every eye is glued on me.

"What?"

"I can't believe you forgot about the dog I gave you, Dorothy?" Lorene frowns. "You are not a responsible pet owner."

Guilty! "Well, I was a bit distracted after the storm."

Lorene's not through fussing at me.

"You left Pepper to fend for himself. What were you thinking?" I have no excuse. Clint was on my mind. I failed Pepper.

Clint says, "There was no time to look for him, Lorene."

He's right, but I'm still ruinously in trouble with her.

Double DD! I inwardly curse, reminded of a Bible verse. *Let the words of your mouth and the meditations of your heart be acceptable unto God.*

"I'm sorry I forgot about Pepper, Lorene," I apologize.

She's still peeved as a server arrives with our menus, a separate one for specialty coffees and teas. Alicia's eyes light up over the choices. "I know what I want," Clint says. "Caffeine straight up."

I am undecided. Lorene orders a vanilla latte and Alicia chooses the almond tea with honey. "I'll have the same as Clint," I say.

Maybe caffeine will clear my head when it comes to him.

"So, Mr. Howard, why did you decide to move to Columbia?" Lorene locks her gaze on me. She's prying and knows I don't like it.

"The job came open and I needed a change," he replies.

"I really enjoy living here," Alicia gushes. "I've found the best friends I've ever had. And the weather's better. Great Britain Isles are cold and damp most of the year. I wonder if the sun will ever shine."

I am seated beside Alicia, so I pat her hand. "We're so glad you're here, but disturbed that so much trouble has fallen at your door."

"Alicia will be fine," Clint says. "The police are competent."

He smiles sweetly at me. I can't help but smile back.

"I think I'll have a cinnamon roll," I declare, thinking some sugar will get my mind off a night of hot sex with the new mystery man.

The camaraderie is pleasant and Clint shares how he grew tired of working and traveling, so decided to settle down quietly. I am watching him closely and wondering if he's lying through his teeth.

How can I love a man I don't trust? *Oh, Arthur!*

Alicia knows a great deal about international teas and gives us a history of how it became so important in British history. The country's nation-building around the world, particularly the Oriental East, is partially responsible for the popularity of tea among British residents.

"I will stick to coffee," Lorene concludes. "I suppose we can also thank the British for the forerunners of coffee houses during the eighteenth century. It took a while to catch on in America."

I glance at the time on my cell phone. "Girls, we need to find a place to have lunch then go back to Lorene's and make some plans."

"What kind of plans?" Clint asks, signaling our server to bring the ticket. He has money and I know the county doesn't pay that well. His job at the Senior Citizen Center may be a cover. For what?

"Thank you for our beverages," I tell Clint.

"My pleasure, ladies. Enjoy your lunch."

On our way out of the restaurant, I feel Clint's large hand slip into my jacket pocket. I dare not reach for it. My heart jitters at the idea of a secret message from a secret-agent handsome man.

Lunch is at McDonald's. We order salads and eat quickly.

We are back at Lorene's house by one thirty when I excuse myself to go upstairs and use the restroom. Only then do I dare reach into my coat pocket to see what Clint has secretly slipped me.

My hands shake as I unfold the note and begin reading. **COME TO MY APARTMENT AT 8 P.M. FOR SUPPER**.

He must know I am suspicious of his motives.

Nevertheless, I was never one to ignore a mystery. Maybe Lorene was right, that I should write a novel instead of living one.

As we end our game of Five Crowns around four p.m., I tell the girls I plan to spend the night with Claire. "What about me?"

The question comes from Alicia.

"You can stay the night with Lorene," I answer. "By tomorrow, the forensic team should be through going over your cabin."

Alicia nods, but I can tell she's nervous about my leaving.

"We'll all be fine," I tell them both. "God is our refuge, right?"

"Right!" they say.

I leave Lorene's house just before dark and drive over to my house. There's a lot of activity going on in and around the property. Dr. Preston walks over as I lower the window on the driver's side.

"Mrs. Powell, Graham has told me so much about you since we've become close," she reveals, and it makes me wonder just how close.

"What's going on at my house?" I inquire.

"A contractor is inside assessing the damage. He'll report to your insurance company and give them an estimated price for repairs," she replies. "Your agent will give you a call and go over all the details."

"I sure wish they'd hurry; I miss my home."

"Repairs could take a few months, Ms. Powell."

"*A few months?*" I nearly shout.

"Lots of damage in Maury County, unfortunately."

"Still, I am hopeful." I always was a dreamer.

"Graham told me you're staying with Ms. Lorene."

"I am." I wonder if marriage for them is possible.

"Is your team finished with Miss Colby's cabin?" I ask.

"Tomorrow, we're still looking around your place."

"Why? I've had no prowlers."

"You aren't aware someone has been sleeping in your shed?" she asks. "We're still looking for fingerprints to identify the squatter."

I am mad at Butch. He never told me.

"Okay, I'll let Alicia know." I resign myself to "It is what it is."

She bangs on the fender. "Nice ride, Ms. Powell."

"Yes, it is." I close the window and decide to drive over to the cabin, remembering curiosity killed the cat, and my date later tonight.

My phone rings. "Oh, hi, Claire."

"Mama, you promised to call. What's going on?"

"I'm fine, worry wort! Is Ted feeling much better?" I recall Claire had to go home last Tuesday to take him to the clinic.

"Yes, but Helen's youngest daughter came down with Covid."

"Oh, no, how sick is June?" She's five and in kindergarten.

"Low-grade fever and a cough, she'll be fine," Claire reports.

"That's good." I have nothing more to say.

"Mama, where are you staying nights?"

"With Lorene. Alicia Colby is also her guest," I reply.

"Why? Her cabin was not damaged from the storm, right?"

"No, but some unusual things are going on," I reply. "She's not comfortable staying alone at the cabin." I won't go into details.

"Come stay with us until your house is repaired," Claire pleads.

I don't answer.

"Okay, I know you won't. You have a life of your own."

She's right, but I don't want to make it an issue between us.

"Are you still spending time with Clint Howard?"

"As a matter of fact, he bought a round of coffees for us girls this morning," I reveal. "He's a real gentleman, and I like him."

"He seems to be," Claire notes. "Just be careful."

"I always am, Claire."

I have yet to tell her that Mark Hagen is on the loose and possibly has spent one or more nights in my shed. And that someone with size nine boots broke in Lorene's house while she was visiting her daughter in Kentucky. Why worry her since the police are investigating?

"Okay, be safe and call soon," Claire says.

"Tell June I will be praying for her."

When the call ends, I drive down the gravel road to the cabin.

I am shocked to see a tattered gray van parked in the driveway. It doesn't belong to the CSI team. They're still busy at my house.

Maybe foolishly, I park in the front yard and walk around the back to assess what's going on. Zoey Jackson is standing there, looking down at something on the ground. "Zoey!" I call out to her.

She glances up, tears clouding her big brown eyes as I approach.

"I'm sorry I haven't called, are you okay?"

"No, my grandaddy's house fell down with me under the bed."

"I'm so sorry." I give her a hug. "I had roof damage. Everything in my den and kitchen area will need to be replaced."

"I saw the mess when I drove past," she tells me.

"Why are you here so late?" I ask the nineteen-year-old.

"I wanted to see if Miss Colby would hire me. The community college is closed until repairs have been made. We're online now."

"She's not coming home tonight; she's with Lorene Perkins."

"Oh." Zoey seems disappointed.

"Where are you staying nights?" I inquire.

"In my grandfather's old van," she replies.

"That junker parked out front? Does it even have heat?"

She shakes her head no. "I'll be okay, Ms. Powell."

I know Zoey is a survivor. She once was a secretary for a mafia ring in Nashville. Her mother is dead, and her father is still serving prison time. Two years ago, her grandfather was murdered.

Yet, with my financial help, Zoey is making positive changes.

"What were you staring at on the ground?" I walk a few steps closer and spy a silver clip that holds cash on the wet ground.

"That wasn't there yesterday," I note.

Zoey reaches to pick up the clip.

"No, don't touch it!" I warn her. "It may be evidence."

Zoey appears troubled. "Evidence for what?"

"Leave your van here and come with me."

"Where?"

I grasp her arm and lead her to my BMW. "You can stay with Lorene Perkins until I can find you a safe shelter."

On our way past my house, I receive a text with Ellie's phone number so I call her. "How is Pepper doing?"

"He's wonderful! I love this little dog."

"Good, because I need for you to keep him a few more days."

"No problem. I'm taking some vacation time anyhow."

"Do I need to drop off dogfood?" I inquire.

"No, I purchased a bag. The vet checked Pepper over and wrote a prescription for worm pills," Ellie informs me.

I forgot he needed a vet visit. I'm a bad dog-owner.

"Don't be concerned; Pepper is getting along marvelously."

"That's good to hear. We'll talk again soon."

We're driving over to Lorene's when Zoey asks, "When can you move back in your home?" Her eyes are ringed in dark circles. I think she may not be sleeping or eating properly. Does she have money?

"Probably not for some time," I reply.

We knock on Lorene's door and Alicia answers.

"Back so soon?" The elderly woman stares at Zoey.

"This is my young friend, Zoey Jackson," I introduce her. "She's homeless and needs shelter. Where is Lorene?"

"She's on the phone talking to Sam about her squatter."

Zoey and I enter the house, and I lead her into the kitchen where I put on a kettle of boiling water to make tea. I find a carton of sweet rolls in the fridge and warm up four for a late-afternoon snack.

"If we eat now, we'll ruin our dinner," Alicia warns.

"It won't ruin mine," Zoey pipes, "I'm starving."

The girl has lost at least five pounds since I've seen her. I wish she'd come to see me before now. I feel responsible for her welfare.

As we sit at the breakfast bar, I query Zoey. "It's been over a week since I've seen you or you've called me. What's going on, dear?"

"I've been hiding," she admits.

"Why?" I ask.

"Before the storm, for three nights, around eleven, the same black van drove past my granddaddy's house," Zoey reveals. "The driver was huge and black. I didn't see his face. It might be Dom."

"Dom?" Alicia repeats. "That's an odd name."

"Who is this Dom?" Her statement worries me.

"A very bad man who used to own a nightclub in Nashville," she replies. "He ran a prostitute ring with Sonja Berioski's help."

"Now, Sonja is a name I recognize," I declare. "I thought the feds ran those folks out of the city. You need to tell Detective Peters."

Zoey sighs and sits back in the barstool. I sense a maybe.

"Thanks for the refreshments," she tells me.

"What did I miss?" Lorene appears in the doorway between the kitchen and the dining rooms. "What's smelling so good?"

"Sweet rolls," I reply. "You remember Zoey?"

"Of course, she's the college student that cleans your house on Tuesdays," Lorene replies while opening the lid to the Styrofoam carton that originally contained sweet rolls. "You didn't save me one?"

"Sorry, Ms. Perkins," Zoey apologizes. "I ate the last one."

"It's okay. I don't need sweets since we're having steaks for supper. Graham and Cynthia will be here around seven thirty."

"Are you still going to Claire's for the night?" Lorene asks me.

"She wants me to come," I say. It's not a lie, but there's more to the story. I have a dinner date with Clint at eight p.m.

"Why is Zoey here?" Lorene asks as she fixes a cup of hot tea.

"Her grandfather's house collapsed in the storm," I reply. "She needs shelter tonight? Tomorrow, I'll find a more permanent living quarters for Zoey until my house is fixed and she moves in with me."

"Sure, no problem," Lorene replies. "The more the merrier."

"Thank you." We still need to discuss this Dom character.

18

GRAHAM ARRIVES WITH CYNTHIA a few minutes before seven p.m.

"Hi, Mom. I see you have company." He eyes the elderly woman with wispy gray hair and withering paper-thin skin. The dark green in her black eyes are most unusual. "Who is this lovely lady?"

"This is Alicia Colby, Clyde Willems' great aunt," Lorene replies, wearing an apron and carrying a big spoon in one hand as she stands at the front door. Alicia steps forward to greet them.

"Pleased to meet you both," Alicia shakes their hands.

"Come on in before you both catch a cold."

"Thank you, Mrs. Perkins, I do hope we're not intruding."

"Oh, no, I can always set another plate for a guest."

Lorene closes the door and locks it.

Graham's expression prompts a response as he assists Cynthia in shedding her short leather coat, hanging hers next to his in the closet tucked under the staircase. Together, they walk into the den.

"As I've said before, dear son, people I don't know show up sometimes without an invitation. We can't be too careful."

"I thought Mrs. Powell was staying with you," the female M.E. comments as the four of them enter the kitchen.

"She's spending the night with her daughter," Lorene reveals.

"You have a beautiful home," Cynthia notes with a smile.

"Crawford and I enjoyed it for a decade." Tears cloud the widow's lemony gaze. "It's too big for one person. I was hoping one of my boys would take it off my hands." She looks at Graham for a decision.

He grasps Cynthia's hand and Lorene notices the big diamond ring on her fourth left finger. "Cyn and I are engaged," he announces.

Cyn is too much like sin for Lorene's liking. It's shocking news.

"We came over tonight for supper to tell you we plan to be married at Thanksgiving." He adoringly looks down at Cyn.

"Isn't this engagement kind of sudden?" Lorene asks before thinking. "You've only been dating, what? Three months."

"We knew from the moment I filled my pharmacy prescription at Walgreen's, Ms. Preston," Cyn reveals with a perfect dental smile.

Graham is a pharmacist, so Cyn's statement made sense to Alicia.

"Where will your ceremony be?" Lorene inquires.

"Here at the house, Mama," Graham replies.

"That's three weeks from now—how can I possibly be ready to receive your guests?" Lorene confronts him with a dose of reality.

"Only our immediate families will be invited," he replies. "Maybe Ms. Powell can help you with the food preparations."

Lorene feels awkward, doesn't know how to respond.

Alicia gushes to save the moment: "Congratulations to both of you! I can't physically contribute, but I will financially."

Lorene turns to Alicia. "That is so sweet, dear, but unnecessary. But, of course, you are invited. I wouldn't dream of celebrating Graham and Cynthia's wedding without my best friends around."

"Mama? Should I put the steaks on the grill?" Grant spies the meat tray on the counter. "It's getting late and I work early tomorrow."

"Of course, son. The baked potatoes are warming in the oven, and I made a green-bean casserole with mushrooms and onions."

"What can I do to help with dinner?" Cynthia inquires.

"Just before we eat, you can fix our beverages—there's sweet tea in the fridge and the dining room table is set. I'll cook the rolls. I left a chair for Dorothy, hoping she won't drive to Nashville tonight."

Graham looks at me for an explanation. "Dorothy is my best friend, son, and I worry about her." That's all he needs to know.

The forensic scientist investigating the break-in at Alicia Colby's cabin cannot avoid asking, "Why is that, Mrs. Perkins?"

"She has too many irons in the fire." Lorene won't mention Dorothy's infatuation with the mystery man, Clint Howard.

"I couldn't help but notice how much time she's spending with the new manager of the Senior Citizen Center," Cyn reports. "What is Ms. Powell—eighty-two years old and counting? Is she dating him?"

"It's none of *our* business, Cynthia," Lorene curtly responds. "Grant, go ahead and fire up the grill and get the steaks going."

"Sure, Mama." He gazes at his fiancée. She's a tiger after the truth and won't let this matter drop. She's already irritated his mother.

The four of them sit down for dinner at 8:15 p.m.

Zoey was tired earlier and said she didn't want supper. She was sleeping upstairs. Another dinner is also in progress in Columbia.

* * *

I park my BMW in the spot marked GUEST in front of Clint's apartment complex and enter the building. Huffing up a flight of stairs to the second level, his door opens before I have a chance to knock.

"I was afraid you wouldn't come," he says, almost frantically.

"Why would you think that? You know I can't avoid a puzzle."

"Let me take your jacket."

Rather than answer my question, he moves behind me to remove my jacket and lingers a bit longer. I'm frozen in place at his closeness.

"You smell delicious," he whispers huskily. *"Chanel?"*

I turn around. "Yes, Arthur liked me wearing that scent."

His cologne is intoxicating, but I will not let him woo me senseless. Tonight, I am determined to get to the root of the truth.

"I smell something good cooking," I put some distance between us. *Don't let him get too close, you old fool,* I warn myself.

He follows me like a lost puppy. I turn around and we lock eyes. His are magnificent, olive-black, with flecks of gold.

"Would you like a glass of wine before dinner?" he inquires.

"Sure." I usually don't imbibe, but tonight is special.

"I have red or white."

"Whatever you're having, Clint."

He exits the room as I sit down on the butter-creamy leather sofa to wait. I've thought about this moment all afternoon—what to say.

Clint returns with my glass of Burgundy. I sip on the beverage and feel it burn my throat as it trickles down. "So, the mystery . . .?"

"Yes, why I've asked you here tonight." The wingback is too small for his large frame. "You're surprised at my invitation. I get that."

I lean back and glare at him. "Are we dating?"

He smiles. "Is that what you want?"

"Why is it you answer questions with a question?"

"I didn't realize I did." His poignant gaze probes me.

"Who are you really?" I point-blank ask.

He sets his wine glass on the coffee table and moves over to the sofa, settling his manicured hands on his knees. "Clint Howard."

"No, you're not!" I turn half-way in my seat to face him.

He smiles. "I told them you'd figure it out."

"Told *who*?" The mystery thickens.

"The people I work for."

"The CIA?"

"No, the Mafia. Particularly, Mark Hagen."

He has my full attention, and I think maybe I should toss the rest of my wine in his face and make a run for the door.

"You jest?"

He chuckles. "Yes, I jest. I'm CIA undercover."

The weight of the world lifts off my shoulders.

"Why are you investigating me?" My feelings are ruffled. "I'm as ordinary as apple pie. And you've tricked me, whoever you are."

"There are some details you should know before you judge me too harshly," he says, "but first let's eat my chicken casserole."

I wonder if I have a choice, so I comply.

We dine at the small square kitchen table overlooking a courtyard behind the apartment complex. The lights of Columbia are sparkling in the dark with the moon hidden from view. Outdoors, myriads of stars are glittering over earth's globe. It's a romantic night for lovers.

So far, I've said nothing. I'm waiting for his confession.

Without speaking, he serves me my portion of casserole. For dessert, we have cherry pie. He knows how I like my decaf coffee, with cream and two sugars. Ignorance was bliss. It was magical believing I am desirable again to a younger man. I help him clear the table and load the dishwasher. I don't want this evening to end.

"You're mighty quiet, Dorothy," he tells me.

"I know." I might not ever see this man again now that the truth is out. Tears are dripping down my cheeks and I'm trembling.

He turns, his hands on my shoulders. "Oh, Dorothy."

I look up at him—all six feet, four inches of him. Those gorgeous olive-black eyes and that full head of thick gray hair.

"I'm sorry." I dry my eyes and try to compose my emotions.

"No, I'm sorry, I really like you. I need to explain."

Before I realize what I'm about to do, I draw his lips to mine and kiss him sweetly. "I needed to do that once, at least."

The kind soul he is, he kisses me firmly on the mouth.

I gently push him away. "I'm not that kind of fool." I will not sleep with him tonight, though I'd really like to be foolish.

19

Thursday, November 3

IT'S AFTER ONE A.M. Thursday morning, and Lorene cannot sleep. She's turned over so many times in bed, she's wrapped in the sheets. The backdoor had shut a good hour ago and she'd checked to see who went out. It was Zoey Jackson leaving. She spied her getting into a yellow Toyota with a young man, her boyfriend, probably.

Kicking off the covers, Lorene climbs out of bed and uses the facilities, wondering if Alicia is also awake. After a glass of O.J. in the kitchen, she tiptoes up the stairs and down the hall to the first bedroom on her right. The door is partially open. "Come on in, Lorene."

"I hope I didn't wake you," she tells Alicia, "I couldn't sleep."

"Is there a problem?"

"Besides not being able to sleep? There might be. You had already gone to bed when Dorothy's daughter phoned around 9:45."

"What did Claire want?" The elderly woman is propped up on pillows in bed and reading her Bible. She closes the Good Book.

"To speak to her mother," Lorene replies. "Dorothy told us she was spending the night with Claire. Do you think she lied?"

"Is it possible she's been involved in a car accident?"

"She would have called us." Lorene perches on the edge of the bed contemplating the situation. "What should I do?"

"Call Claire back and tell her the truth," Alicia says.

"What if she's with Clint Howard?"

"Yes, I saw how he made eyes with Dorothy while we were together at Coffee Call. He's too young for her, and with all the shenanigans going on around Columbia, I don't trust him."

Alicia closes the Good Book and stretches.

"I'll phone Claire back and see if Dorothy's arrived," Lorene decides. "It will make us both feel better so maybe we can sleep."

Lorene removes her cell phone from her housecoat pocket and finds her list of contacts. Claire Burkes' number is keyed in. She punches the digits and the phone rings several times.

"No answer," she tells Alicia.

"Normal people are asleep at this time of night, let it ring."

Finally, a "Hello."

"Is this Claire?"

"No, this is Ted, who's calling?"

"It's me, Lorene Perkins. May I speak to Dorothy."

She hears mumblings, then another salutation, "This is Claire."

"Claire, this is Lorene, I need to speak to Dorothy."

"She's not here—did she say she was coming over?"

"Yes, I last saw her late this afternoon. She said she was driving to Nashville and spending the night with you," Lorene explains, now worried that something terrible has happened to Dorothy.

"If that's the case, she didn't make it."

"Do you know about Mark Hagen?" Lorene asks.

"The serial killer—he's in prison."

"No, he isn't. He escaped over a month ago."

"Do you think he's after my mother because she turned him in?" Claire asks as hysteria fills her voice. "I should call the police."

"Wait! I have no proof! Besides, she has to be missing twenty-four hours before they will look for her," Lorene says.

"What should I do?"

Lorene can hear alarm in Claire's voice.

"I think I know a place she may have gone."

The silence over the airways is chilling.

"That man's place," Claire says.

"She's pretty hung up on Clint Howard."

"Will you call him and see if Mama's there?" Claire asks.

"Sure, then I'll call you back."

Lorene ends the call and stares at Alicia.

"She's in trouble, I knew it. Women have that sixth sense."

* * *

We're at my house with Clint when his phone rings. He looks at the Caller I.D. "It's your friend, Lorene. Should I talk to her?"

"She'll think it's odd if you don't."

His lips wiggle with amusement.

"What? Lorene has probably figured out by now that I'm not spending the night with Claire," I say. "Answer it."

"Hello." He puts his phone on SPEAKER so I can hear.

"Mr. Howard, this is Lorene Perkins, I'm looking for Dorothy."

"What's going on, Lorene?" Clint winks at me, like it's a game he's enjoying. I want to slug him.

"She was supposed to be spending the night with her daughter, but I just talked to Claire, and she isn't there. I'm worried sick."

"I don't know what to tell you, Lorene," he replies.

"When did you last see her?"

"At Coffee Call this morning." He winks at me again.

"Should I call the police? Is it possible she returned home?"

Clint says, "If it will make you feel any better, I'll drive over there and see," he offers. "How 'bout I text you if I locate her?"

"That would be wonderful! I'll wait for your call."

Clint pockets his phone.

"She's worried something's happened to you," he tells me.

"I'll phone her later," I decide.

"Your call." He smiles.

"Exactly what am I looking for?"

Clint has already told me everything. Mark Hagen killed his wife and only son twenty years ago. He never remarried and worked for the Central Intelligence Agency overseas for the most part of his law-enforcement career. After growing up and graduating high school in Murfreesboro, he attended Tulane in New Orleans and earned a degree in Law Enforcement. He also speaks Russian fluently. One huge surprise: Mark Hagen's escape from prison was planned by the CIA.

"You're looking for anything that Clyde Willems gave Arthur," Clint replies. "From our intel, we believe Clyde kept a list of people involved with the Russian Mafia in four states. He knew he was in trouble and death was imminent, so he gave Arthur the information."

"Clyde worked for Arthur, but they weren't really friends," I say.

"They played poker together every Friday night."

"And Arthur lent him money, so maybe there was trust between them—why didn't you ask these questions two years ago when he died? And poor Crawford Perkins was caught in the crossfires."

Clint flashes his cell phone over the den, too cluttered for us to walk through. "Dorothy, please think. Did Arthur ever receive a gift from Clyde?" He pauses. "We need to locate that information."

"I'm tired. Let's go out on the front porch and sit down. I need to think about that." I'm still upset Clint has toyed with my heart.

As we sit on the front porch steps and stare up at the stars, I feel all mushy inside with Clint seated so close to me. I realize I've fallen in love with the idea of love, which is not real, and can never be real. I am too old for Clint, rather *Thomas Kessler*, his real name.

As he grasps my hand and pats it, a flash of memory courses my mind. "Wait! On Arthur's last birthday, Clyde gave him a book."

"That's it!" Clint jumps up, excited. "Where is the book?"

"I donated it to the public library eighteen months ago."

"What was the name of the book?" Clint inquires.

"Let me think." I try to picture the front of the book with its title. "I don't recall, but the librarian may have a record of my gift."

"Okay, we'll go to the library when it opens tomorrow morning."

"Where will we sleep?"

"Let's go back to my apartment, you can stay in the guest bedroom," he says, tugging at my arm to help me get up.

"Lorene will be worried if you don't call her back and tell her you found me," Dorothy says. I am concerned over how *this* looks.

"Up to you." Clint looks down at me.

The drive seems brief in light of my heavy thoughts. I worry that my daughter will find out what I'm doing. And if Lorene and Alicia have figured out that I lied to them, they might never forgive me.

The town at night is quiet, especially after the awful storms that blew through. Clint pulls into a garage underneath his apartment.

The gentleman in him opens the passenger door for me.

"Thank you." I look up at him, probably dreamily.

He smiles back. "You're something, Dorothy."

Yes, I am, I think. *But not your girlfriend.*

As I close the blinds in Clint's guest bedroom, I wish our story had turned out differently. I was happy thinking he was single, a newcomer to town, and interested in dating me. I lay on my back in the bed staring up at the ceiling for a long time. Broken hearts are difficult to negotiate. Mine hasn't been broken since I was in the fifth grade and found out that Scooter Boots didn't like me back.

"Oh, Arthur," I mutter and turn over in the bed, thinking if I die tonight, it would not be so bad. Heaven has no broken hearts.

20

Friday, November 4

ELLIE LET LLOYD SPEND the night at her apartment, but he slept on the sofa. Her mother had phoned twice yesterday to ask questions about plans for their wedding. She's told her, "Lloyd wants to keep the ceremony simple and invite only family and a few friends."

He was still snoring on the sofa when she put on the coffee. Pepper was yelping at her feet because he wanted to go out and pee.

"Lloyd, wake up and take the dog out for a walk!" she called out.

"Huh." He groggily sits up, despising he drank that third can of Budweiser before falling asleep on the sofa last night. It wasn't the romantic evening he'd envisioned. Ellie was sticking to her plan. No sex until they were married. He was counting off the weeks.

"Get up and take Pepper out to pee," she orders. "I'll make you bacon, eggs, and toast for breakfast before you take off for work."

Lloyd throws his legs off the sofa and glares at Ellie. His chin itches from hair stubbles, and his stomach burns with acid. He feels awful and needs caffeine to wake up. "Any coffee made?"

"It will be ready by the time you come back in," she says.

"You're killing me, Ellie. Once a man has drank from the well, he gets mighty thirsty often." He doesn't know if he can wait that long.

She sassily places a hand on one hip and grins. "I love the sexy way you talk to me. I promise when we get married, you won't get thirsty." She returns to the kitchen to nuke the bacon in a microwave.

"Come on, Pepper." Lloyd snags the terrier and off they go.

Thirty minutes later, he has showered and dressed for work. He sits at the breakfast bar beside Ellie munching on crisp bacon. "The eggs taste fresh. Did they come from the Farmer's Market?"

"Yes, they did. And my biscuits are homemade. I'm practicing being a good wife." She glances over at him. "I keep my promises."

"You better." He pinches her on the arm. "I need you to come into the office today," he mumbles with a mouthful of scrambled eggs.

"My vacation isn't over, Lloyd."

"I'll give you one day off next week, okay?"

"What do you want me to do?" Ellie takes a bite of toast. She's on a diet to lose five more pounds so she can fit in her grandmother's antique-white wedding dress. White is for virgins—she's not one.

"Look cute and pay some bills." Lloyd winks. "I have an appointment with the Tennessee Special Agent in charge of the investigation into Lorita Willem's murder. He phoned yesterday."

"A new development in her murder case?"

"Captain Colbert has decided to fill me in on the whole shebang." Lloyd brushes bread crumbs from his hands. "I need to go now."

"Okay, I'll shower and be in the office by ten. First, I need to call Dorothy Powell to see if she can watch Pepper for the day," Ellie says.

"If Dorothy doesn't answer her phone, call Lorene Perkins." He shakes his head. "There're like two peas in a pod." Then chuckles.

"Okay." Ellie sweetly kisses her fiancé. "You know I love you."

"Showing me is better." He plants a lingering kiss on her mouth. "Just so you don't forget what a great lover I am. See you at the office."

Pepper sits on the bathroom floor watching Ellie shower. He's such a great little guy it will be nice to have a big back yard where he can frolic and play. Ellie has her eye on a specific property, thinking Dorothy might repair her 1934 farmhouse and decide to sell it. After all, the woman isn't getting any younger and will eventually need someone to care for her physical needs. Ellie sighs. One can hope.

* * *

The Maury Public Library opens its doors on Fridays at eight a.m. Clint and Dorothy are seated in his Ford Taurus waiting for someone to unlock the front door. Lucy Pennetta pokes her head out the door and calls out to them, "We're closed today for inventory."

I get out of the car and mount the library steps. "Lucy, my friend Clint and I really need to speak with you about a matter."

"What matter?" Lucy, pencil-thin with a wrinkled face and mousy-blond hair, clings to the door like she's guarding the National Archives.

"It's a police matter," I reply.

Lucy draws her face back in her neck like a ruffled hen. "You're not a law officer, need I remind you." She glares at Clint in the car.

"It's important to a murder case." I need to give Lucy a reason to admit us to the library and answer our pertinent questions.

"Is he an agent for TBI?" Her gaze is penetrating.

"More international," I share.

"Okay then." She crooks a finger at Clint. He sticks his long legs out of the car, gets out and approaches. "Thank you, Lucy."

"Have we met?" Lucy asks.

"Yes, at the Senior Citizen Center," he replies with a brilliant grin.

That dog can charm the pants off a woman, I think to myself.

"I'm the new manager. May we come inside?"

I shake my head at Lucy: *Don't tell him what I told you.*

She understands it's our secret and slyly winks.

"Sure, Mr. Howard." Lucy recalls his name.

"Clint, please."

Lucy locks the library door and we are alone with her in the hallows of history. There is every kind of book written in this facility.

"I just made coffee in the kitchen. Would you like a cup?"

"Thank you, Lucy," he says and follows her.

I have never seen the librarian so friendly. With Clint's good looks and schmoozing techniques, plus his undercover status, Lucy is like putty in his hands. I stand back amazed at watching him work.

This is my first time inside the kitchen. It is spotless, reflecting the organized mind of our librarian. Lucy fills three mugs with coffee.

"The cream and sugar are on the table," she tells me.

"Thank you, Lucy."

We sit down and Clint tells Lucy about my book gift to the library approximately six months after Arthur died. "That would be in April, eighteen months ago," he pinpoints the month. "Could you check?"

"So, you want me to identify the specific titles Dorothy donated to the library?" She peers at him, then me. "May I ask why?"

Clint locks eye with me, signaling I need to come up with a plausible reason to put Lucy to so much trouble. I'm stupefied a moment before my creative brain takes charge of my mouth.

"Clyde Willems gave Arthur a gift, and Clint thinks it's pertinent to a murder case Detective Peters is working on," I reply.

"Clyde Willems' half-sister in Dickson?"

I know Lucy has read about the case.

"We hate to put you to so much trouble," I add.

"Luckily, we back up our donations for five years," she tells us. "Meanwhile, enjoy your coffees while I go to my office and check."

He grasps my hand. "That was perfect, Dorothy."

"Thank you. Butch knows I'm a good investigator," I brag.

"Detective Lloyd Peters?"

"Yes, everyone called him Butch when he was in high school. I still don't like him because he groped by daughter when she was a freshman. He's apologized, but a mother never forgets a bad deed."

His lips wiggle. "Then, I better make sure I'm not bad."

He's flirting again. If I had a gun, I'd shoot him.

We drink our coffees in silence while we wait for Lucy to return. She is gone only fifteen minutes. "Here's the list." She hands it to me.

"Thank you, Lucy, we'll get out of your hair now," I say.

Clint stands and faces Lucy. "If you don't mind, keep what we've said and done here this morning between the three of us. Okay?"

"No problem, my lips are sealed."

On our way out the front door, with the book list tucked inside my purse, I comment to Clint, "You've won another heart. Shame on you!" I am as seriously annoyed and jealous of the woman who will eventually woo his heart. I wish that woman could be me.

In response, he elbows me. "You're fun, you know that, Dorothy Powell!" We approach his car. "Under other circumstances . . ."

He doesn't complete his sentence.

"I know, if I were seventeen years younger," I complete his thought. "But I'm not, so let's keep this relationship on a business level." I've decided to work hard on protecting my heart.

"Where to now?" I ask as we drive through Columbia.

"I'll drop you off at Lorene's. I have work to do," he replies.

"Okay." I may have to lie about where I spent the night.

The drive takes twenty minutes. I instruct Clint to let me out at the end of the drive and I'll walk the rest of the way to the house.

"Will I see you again?"

"Of course!" he hails. "We're buddies, right?"

"Right." I frown as I start the steep walk up the drive.

Claire's beige Buick is parked in front of Lorene's house. I am in trouble. I don't knock, rather push open the door and step inside.

"I'm home, honey!" I facetiously call out.

Seconds later, three people are up close and in my face.

"Mama! I'm going to kill you. Where have you been?"

Lorene and Alicia don't have friendly smiles. They are aggravated at me, too. What can I say? I spent the night with a gorgeous man. We're solving a crime together and probably going to put some criminals behind bars. Instead, my lips are tied as Claire hugs me so tightly that I can't get my breath. And Pepper is jumping at my feet.

"We forgive you," Alicia says, "and grateful you're okay."

* * *

"Who's watching Dorothy's dog?" Lloyd asks when Ellie is seated at her desk. He glances at the wall clock. TBI Special Agent in Charge Stanley Kilpatrick should be here any moment now. "The dog, Ellie?"

She stops typing, "Pepper's spending the day with Lorene."

"Are you picking him up this afternoon?"

"I could . . . what do you have in mind?"

"A Friday Date Night, sugar."

"Okay, I'm sure Lorene won't mind another overnight guest."

She continues paying bills electronically, hoping some hacker doesn't steal their money. "And what is the agenda, *sugar*?"

"We can go back to your apartment for a nightcap."

She stops tying and looks at him hard. "You never give up."

"That's a good thing!" Stanley Kilpatrick hails as he stands loosely at the office door, arms crossed. "May I enter your inner sanctum?"

"Agent Kilpatrick!" Lloyd hails out of respect. "Coffee?"

"No, thanks. Can we speak privately in your office?"

"Sure." Lloyd eyes Ellie. They have no secrets between them.

"Have a seat." Lloyd motions to Stan as soon as his office door is closed. "What's up?" He takes a seat at his desk.

"Marilyn Colbert and I think you should see the whole picture," Stan begins. "Have you met Clint Howard?"

"The new manager of the Senior Citizen Center, yeah, why?"

"He's CIA undercover. They have an interest in Mark Hagen since his criminal activities are international. Clint's been keeping an eye on Dorothy Powell, hoping she possesses information that will bring down the Russian Mafia bosses in four states: Tennessee, Arkansas, Mississippi, and Kentucky. Nashville is a throughway for drug trafficking and prostitution. Mark Hagen's escape was planned."

Lloyd attempts to absorb all the information at once, many questions surfacing. "Is Mrs. Powell in danger?"

"Yes. Mark hired Clint to kidnap her," Stan replies.

"Has he told her that?"

"I doubt it." Stan crosses his legs. "He likes her."

"Romantically?" Lloyd is surprised.

"She's the spitting image of his first wife. Hagen murdered her and their fourteen-year-old son twenty years ago. Clint has never remarried and carries a vengeance that's destroyed his happiness. Even I'm not sure of his real identity. His creds are impeccable."

Lloyd shrugs. This is new information and changes everything.

"The agent is blown away by Dorothy's resemblance to his wife."

Lloyd comments, "Isn't he much younger?"

"Sixty-five and she's eighty-two, but there is no book written that defines the affairs of the heart. Clint will do his job, but he'll make sure Dorothy is safe." A pause. "Even if it kills him."

Lloyd has no comment. He was told to involve Dorothy with Lorita Willems' murder case, and now he understood why. At the time, he didn't realize he had directed her straight into the eye of a storm.

"What can I do to help, Agent Kilpatrick?"

"The plan is about to get sticky," Stan says, then explains why.

As Lloyd listens, he worries about Dorothy's safety.

"I'll do what I can," he agrees.

"Good! I'll be in touch."

The office door opens and Ellie is standing there.

"She won't talk—we're getting married at Christmas," Lloyd defends Ellie's integrity. "Have a great day, Agent Kilpatrick!"

"Wow!" Ellie comments. "That's the stuff of a novel."

21

CLINT STUDIES THE LIST of book titles Lucy Pennetta gave Dorothy. There are twenty, mostly historical fiction. Likely purchased by Arthur or a family member who knew his preference in reading. One title stands out: *The Secret Garden.* Isn't that a children's novel?

Clint puts down the list. It is the only book that doesn't fit Arthur's persona. Lucy had said all donated books after one year were placed on the free-book table. So, who has *The Secret Garden?*

He would need to return to the library and ask Lucy for a list of parents that regularly frequented the library with their young children. The search for that one particular title might turn out ridiculously hard.

Still, he had to try. But he would need Dorothy's help. He looked at the time. Noon, he wonders if she's had lunch yet. He retrieves his cell phone from the jacket on his belt and calls her number.

"Hello."

It isn't Dorothy. He takes a guess, "Claire?"

"Yes, who is this?"

"Clint Howard, is Dorothy around?"

"Haven't you caused her enough trouble? I heard you kidnapped my mother and took her out to the house against her will? Then you refused to let her call anyone. Are you insane?"

Clint inwardly chuckles at Dorothy's ingenuity.

"It didn't quite happen that way. She's safe now, isn't she?"

"Why, I could file a legal complaint against you, Mr. Howard," Claire barks, on a soapbox to defend her mother's honor.

"I don't think Dorothy would agree to that since I needed her help with a matter. She's not mad at me, ask her?" He plays along.

"I already did." The wind goes out of Claire's sails.

"Please leave her alone."

"Is she there?"

"I'm here," I grab the phone from Claire.

"Have you eaten lunch yet?"

"No, what do you have in mind?"

"I need your help with another matter," he says, certain that Claire is listening to their conversation. "I promise not to kidnap you."

I turn away from Claire to hide my smile.

"Where shall I meet you?"

"Same place as usual." He ends the call.

I turn around and glare at Claire. "You don't have to worry, Clint will not hurt me," I assure my adoring daughter.

"Don't go near him, Mama."

"Claire . . ." I grasp her shoulders, "there are things I cannot tell you, other than Butch asked me to assist him in an investigation."

"Mama!"

I walk into the hall and remove my jacket from the closet.

"Whatever you're planning, don't."

"I promise to call you if I'm not back by supper time."

"I can't stay here all day, I have to go home," Claire says.

"Okay, the cell towers work in Nashville, too."

"Don't be cute with me, Mama. You always manage to bump into danger, even when you're being careful. I'm getting gray hair."

"Color it, I did mine." I retrieve my purse off the floor and walk to the front door. Claire trails me like a Mama hawk.

"Oh, I almost forgot, tell Lorene and Alicia that I'm running an errand. I don't want them to worry."

I step outdoors and feel the pleasant breeze flowing from the south. It's a clear blue day as I get in my BMW. I feel optimistic.

And, bless my soul, life is about to get exciting again.

I drive into town and park in front of the apartment complex where Clint stays, reminding myself his living quarters are short-lived. At some point, he will leave me and go back to his old life.

The door to his apartment stands open. "I hope sandwiches and chips are doable since it's all I could put together on short notice."

"Fine, I skipped breakfast," I say as I enter his compact living room and dump my heavy purse on the coffee table. I've started carrying everything imaginable in it, just in case. . .

My thought fades as Clint peeks around the doorjamb and says, "I'm hungry, Dorothy, let's eat then we'll do some work."

I choose sweet ice tea while Clint ravages two ham-and-cheese sandwiches. Just watching him eat is a pleasure, and I'm reminded of how nice it was when Arthur and I sat down to share a meal.

Dare I dream of sharing dining experiences on a regular basis with someone I love? That thought also slips away as Clint looks hard at me.

"Penny for your thoughts?"

"Not worth that much," I tell him then admit, "Actually, I was thinking of my late husband, how nice it was to sit down to a meal with him. You are kind like he was. And bring to me warm memories."

Clint grins. "That's nice, Dorothy. A real nice compliment." He brushes bread crumbs from his hands and picks up his paper plate.

"I'll wait here. Come back and tell me what's developed in the case," I call out, feeling like a real undercover agent working with the greatest guy that must have ever been employed by the CIA.

A few minutes later, I hear the coffeemaker bubble out. I go into the kitchen to add cream and sugar to mine, but Clint says, "I got it, Dorothy." He hands me my mug. "Enjoy your perfect cup of Folgers."

"You remember. Thank you, that's so sweet."

He takes a lingering sip of his coffee. "I went over the list of books you donated to the library," he explains. "One title caught my attention." He motions with his head toward the living room.

Taking his cue, I lead the way, mug in hand. We make a good team. We sit together on the sofa, his hip bumping against mine.

"What is so special about one title?" I ask.

"*The Secret Garden*: would Clyde give Arthur a children's novel?"

"I don't know." I recall the birthday gift was wrapped. "He must have opened it when I was not around. But that is odd."

"I want to talk to the parents who frequent the library with their children. Maybe Lucy has a list of guests the day books were given away. We can call around and see if we can locate that title."

"You think there is a secret code in the book?"

Clint smiles. "You are a quick study and remind me of my wife."

"Your *dead* wife?" I am taken aback by the comparison.

"Yes, you look like her." He removes a photo of Angela and his son Paul and shows it to me. "Your eyes are the same."

I stare at a picture of Angela that could be me thirty-five years ago. She has red hair and Robin-blue eyes. The picture shakes in my hand as I realize this is the reason Clint has been paying attention to me.

I give back his photo. "Why are you telling me this now?"

"I want to come clean. You deserve the truth."

"And what is the truth?"

"I care about you." He puts his arm around me.

I push him away, "No, Clint, you are in love with a memory. I'm not Angela. I'm an old woman that used to look like your deceased wife." Truth can be hard. "Romance for us is not in the future."

"How can you say that, Dorothy? I see the way you look at me."

"I can say that because I'm not foolish, and I like you. We can be friends. We can be partners in crime. Anything but lovers."

Clint settles into the sofa, frowning. "I'm sorry."

"No, dear." I regret my harshness. "I'm glad you are honest with me." The dynamics of my heart deny every word I've said to him.

He takes a sip of coffee. "Let's go down to the library."

"Your call."

The drive over to the library is brief and we aren't talking. What has transpired between us changes our relationship. I have to be careful not to signal I want him in my life as a lover. It's wrong.

Lucy is taking a lunch break so I speak with Lola, one of her newer assistants. "Is there a list of guests that come to the library on free-book-day give-away?" That statement in itself is a mouthful.

"I don't think so," Lola replies.

"Would you check, please."

Lola's eye is on Clint as he stands behind me.

"Oh, this is the new director of the Senior Citizen Center, Clint Howard," I introduce him. "We're looking for a particular book."

"What is the book title?"

"*The Secret Garden*," I reply.

"Oh, that is a fanciful story for children," she declares. "In fact, we have several copies on the shelf. Would you like to see them?"

"Yes, please." I turn around and wink at Clint.

"We can't possibly be that lucky," he whispers over my shoulder. Just being near him sends shivers down my spine. I love him.

"Here, on the bottom shelf." Lola kneels and removes five copies. "Take them over to the table and look through them."

"We will, and thanks," Clint tells Lola.

I thumb through the first copy and glance at the back of the book. There is a page inserted with a list of the names of the children who have read the book. I'm on book five when I notice something odd.

"Look at this, Clint." I show him the last blank page with a scribbled note that says: *Too many circled words, cumbersome.*

Clint thumbs through the book. "I think this is what we're looking for." He notes circled words throughout the book. "Is it possible Clyde named some of his Mafia associates by circling words?"

"I don't know." My blue eyes scan his handsome face. "I'll check out the book, then we'll go through it and write down the circled words. I doubt they are in any order. Possibly, a key to decipher."

"That's my guess, too, let's go," he says.

We return to Clint's apartment and begin our work. An hour and fifteen minutes later, we've recorded thirty-two words, and none of them are proper nouns. I'm discouraged as Clint paces the living room.

"What are you thinking?"

"A code within a code," he declares. "We need to read the entire story and find a clue to the puzzle." He holds up the closed book.

"Like, ever so many words are important?"

"Yes, Clyde was a soldier in World War II. Maybe he used a code like the Germans did to hide their plans from the Americans."

"This is becoming quite complicated." I glance at the time. "I need to go back to Lorene's. Or I'll need to lie again to my best friends about what I've been doing. Thank you for lunch. I know my way out."

"I'll contact the CIA Director and see if he can put me in touch with someone familiar with the German code system," he tells me.

"Okay. You be safe."

"That goes two ways."

I leave his apartment, feeling sad that I've lied to him. Any woman my age would fall into his embrace without forethought. I know he cares for me so what's wrong with my telling him I feel the same way?

"I know . . ." I mutter as I exit the building and get in my car. "It won't work. It won't last. And it's stupid to think I'm Angela."

22

Monday, November 7

TOMORROW I HAVE TO go vote. I haven't heard from Clint all weekend. He's upset with me. Maybe I'll never see him again. I've been so busy solving mysteries that I've failed to check on June. Claire said she tested positive for Covid, the Delta variant. I am a terrible great-grandma. My guilt is as heavy as my expanding belly. In fact, I have eaten far too much since Clint came into my life. I need to diet.

I crawl out of bed in Lorene's upstairs guest bedroom. I listen for noises and decide Alicia is still sleeping or she's gone down stairs. I wonder what time it is. Dark out the window, so still early.

I kick off the covers and toddle down the hall to the bathroom. Light shines from under the door. *Alicia.* I wait, hoping I want mess my pajama bottoms. I hear the shower going. Oh, no, I can't wait.

I rush back to the bedroom and put on my housecoat and slippers. No athlete could move faster as I run down the hall and grab the banister to the stairway. It's dark downstairs as I make my way through the den and through a hallway to the half bath. Glory! It's empty.

There is no greater relief than a good tinkle, I can tell you that.

By the time I get back to the kitchen, Lorene has turned on the lights and is brewing coffee. "You shouldn't run, Dorothy, you're too old. What if you fall and break a leg? You don't even have a house."

"Don't remind me." I'm not a happy camper this morning.

"Isn't your insurance adjuster supposed to get back to you today about house repairs?" my good friend asks, probably tired of guests.

"Yes, but Alicia and I can try to get a hotel room if you need your privacy." I melt in a chair at the bar, waiting to be served coffee.

"No need, what are your plans for today?" She sets a mug in front of me then grabs the cream from the fridge and sugar from the cabinet.

"I haven't been awake long enough to think about that." I take a big sip of Starbuck's and decide that I like Clint's Folgers better.

Or is it his company?

"Your friend hasn't called," Lorene says as she walks around the bar and sits down next to me. She wants intimate details. I won't give it to her, nor anyone else. My private hell is solely my own. It's a battle of flesh against the Christian principles I've employed for most of my life. My mama warned me that men were alluring. Now that I'm older, I wonder if she spoke from personal experience. She'd been married to my daddy for almost sixty years before he passed. Their love must have been strong, because she grieved herself to death in the next four months. Which makes me wonder if I loved Arthur enough.

"You're mighty quiet this morning," Lorene notes.

"Just tired." I sigh and gulp some more coffee.

"Good morning!"

It's bright-and-cheery Alicia and I want to slap her. How dare she be so joyful when I am so miserable. I'm going to call Clint. I can't stand that he's avoiding me. Then a terrible thought. Maybe he can't.

I nearly leap from the bar chair.

"Where are you going?" Lorene asks.

"To run an errand—good morning, Alicia." I rush past her and mount the stairs like I'm going to a fire sale. I need to see if Clint is okay. Once in my car I phone his cell. There's no answer.

He's probably sleeping.

Am I reading too much into his not calling me over the weekend? He has another life. A CIA agent is a busy person. But still, I have to see for myself if he's at the apartment. So, I drive way too fast.

My phone rings as I pull into a GUEST parking space outside Clint's apartment. It's Claire. I don't want to talk to her. I don't want to lie to her if she asks me what I'm doing. So, I don't answer.

I knock on Clint's apartment door. No response.

I lean my ear against the door and listen for sounds.

"What are you doing?"

I turn around and face a squatty man with a bald head and intimidating black eyes that remind me of a mad bull. "Who are you?"

"I was about to ask you the same question, young lady!"

I can't help but smile. He called me young. I'm flattered.

"If you've come to visit the gentleman in that apartment, he's not there," the man says. "I'm the apartment manager, Jenkins."

"Is that a first or last name?" I inquire.

"Last. Guy turned in his key this morning so he's not coming back," Jenkins tells me. "Can I assist you with something?"

My tongue is so tight in my mouth the scream is caught in my throat. I want to kick down the door and deny that Clint, or Thomas Kessler, has moved out of his apartment over the weekend and not even bothered to call me. If that is love, it stinks. I hate him.

There are tears running down my cheeks as I exit the apartment building. I'm responsible for my feelings. I've let him come into my life and take over. What did I expect? He'd call and propose marriage.

There is nothing like an old fool. I hear a crash of thunder.

"Oh, joy! Just what we need, another storm."

I drive back to Lorene's house in hard rain and pure misery. I can't even share my disappointment with my two best friends. I recall that Clint has said more than once to trust him. *Should I?*

The rain slithers down my windshield so fast my wipers are ineffective. I can barely see through the fog gathering around me.

When I last spoke to Clint, he was going to talk to the CIA Director about the German code used during World War II. Perhaps, he'd returned to his office and is busy decoding the message Clyde Willems hid in *The Secret Garden*. Maybe it's premature to judge him so harshly. He may call yet. My hope returns and I realize that's dangerous. It sets me up for another fall, another disappointment.

* * *

Thomas Kessler is in the Washington DC CIA office early Monday morning. When Director Jack Carlton called early Saturday and told him a flight to DC has been arranged, he'd decided not to tell Dorothy. Besides, she'd pretty much blown him off after learning she looked like his deceased wife, Angela. He didn't like it, but Dorothy was right that their age difference was bound to destroy any romantic entanglement. But he missed her. Terribly. But she was out of his life.

The circled words in *The Secret Garden* had a pattern. They were thirteen spaces apart. Using the German Code Book, Jack had come up with four words: garden, four, close, and *flower*. Another agent was assigned to return to Columbia, Tennessee, and locate the fourth row in the garden that had grown flowers behind Clyde Willems' old cabin.

Alicia Colby's prowler had obviously been looking for the spot Clyde designated in the children's book. By now, the garden area was overgrown with weeds and unrecognizable, so Charlie would need to talk to Dorothy Powell to see if she could identify the exact location.

Hopefully, there was buried treasure there. The names of the four Mafia bosses in four states. Having gone to that much trouble, Clyde will certainly have detailed information regarding their operations.

He spied Jack standing in the open doorway.

"Good morning, Director."

"Have you contacted Mark Hagen yet?"

"I was about to." Tom sits up straight in his chair. "How am I going to explain my failure to bring Dorothy Powell to him?"

"You should have." Jack pulls up a chair and sits in it backwards. He is a tall muscular guy, approaching sixty, and sly as they come.

"I know, but I couldn't guarantee he wouldn't hurt her."

Jack shakes his head. "This is about her looking like Angela."

Tom had hoped Jack wouldn't find out. He'd volunteered for the job, claiming he wanted to see Hagen suffer for killing his wife and son twenty years before. Which was true. That Dorothy resembled Angela was never mentioned. "How did you find out?" He sucked in a breath.

"Charlie saw the photo," Jack replied. "What were you thinking, Agent? That you could recall the past and find some comfort?"

"I don't know, Director," Tom admits.

"Well, don't let me catch you communicating with this woman again. I'm sending you on an assignment out of the country."

Tom nods. He was sixty-five. One more assignment and he is retiring. The CIA cannot tell him what to do after that.

* * *

It has rained all day in southern Middle Tennessee. Lorene invited Lizzy over to play cards with them during the afternoon. They were seated at a card table Lorene set up, teaching Alicia how to play Canasta. She claimed to be great at Bridge but Dorothy found it difficult to teach new tricks to an old dog. But they enjoyed the game.

Around four thirty, the four of them are hungry.

"It's still storming. Lizzy, why don't you stay the night?"

"Who will sleep with her?" I ask.

"She can bunk with me, Dorothy," Lorene replies.

"Are you sure?" Lizzy asks in a frail voice. "I could call my daughter and get her to fetch me. I certainly don't want to drive in this inclement weather. I sure hope we don't have tornadoes again."

"Don't even suggest that!" Alicia exclaims.

"I'll order two large pizzas from Domino's," Lorene says.

"And I'll pay for our dinner, you've done quite enough for me and Alicia," I chime in, trying my best to get *alias* Clint out of my mind.

"You don't have to do that," Lorene says.

"My pleasure, don't deny me the opportunity."

My cell phone rings. It startles me. *Is it Clint?*

"Excuse me, I need to take this call," I say. "Hello," I whisper as I step into the foyer for privacy.

"This is Henry Clamper," the male voice announces. "I'm an adjuster for All State Insurance Company."

"I don't know you. Where is Jeff Pauley, my agent?"

"He had a death in his family, Ms. Powell."

"Oh. I'm sorry to hear that. Do you have a quote for repairing my house?" I ask. "I'm anxious to get it fixed so I can move back in."

"Yes, I do. But not everything damaged is covered," he explains. "Would it be possible to meet me at the house tomorrow morning?"

"What time?"

"Eight is good, or we could do it tonight."

"In this kind of weather, no thanks," I tell him.

"Well, it's your option, Ms. Powell. I could get the legal stuff out of the way first thing in the morning if we take care of this tonight."

Tonight. My lips twist in thought.

I walk over to the front door and open it. I can see color as the sun is setting. "Call me in an hour," I tell Mr. Clamper. "If the sky clears, I'll drive over to my house and meet you." It will be a relief.

"Sure. I'll get back to you."

He ends the call and I feel odd about his suggestion. I have no electricity in the house, yet he wants to show me a damaged area that is not covered by my insurance. I should talk to Claire first.

23

I WAS ABOUT TO CALL Claire when Lorene runs out on the porch screaming, "Oh, my Lord! Alicia has fallen down the stairs."

Stunned, I turn around and drop my phone on the porch landing. "Is she hurt bad?" I am already hurrying back into the house.

"I don't know!" Lorene cries. "She's knocked out. I think she hit her head on one of the steps—I've already dialed 9-1-1. What should we do?" I have never seen my best friend so upset.

"We don't move her," I recall a class I took at the Senior Citizen Center. "She could have broken her neck." I need to see Alicia.

She's lying against the bottom step in a crumpled position. Her neck is twisted to one side and leaning against the second step going up. Lorene stands nearby, startled, hands covering her mouth.

"What if she dies? I won't be able to live in this house without seeing her lying helplessly on my staircase!" Lorene cries profusely.

I take a moment to step away from Alicia and hug Lorene. "It will be okay; she's still breathing." We both hear sirens approaching.

"That will be the emergency people. I'll let them in the house." Lorene unsteadily walks to the foyer to greet them.

"In here," I hear her instruct the EMS team as I stand looking down at Alicia, praying her injuries are not as bad as it appears.

"Whose phone is this?" a young tech holds up my cell.

"Mine," I say, "I must have dropped it on the porch."

"Step back, ladies, so we can work," the guy carrying one end of a stretcher hollers out. Lorene and I back off and watch.

A young technician wearing a white cotton shirt and pants takes my information regarding the patient. In the next few minutes, a harness is wrapped around Alicia's neck. She is placed on her back on the stretcher and hauled out the front door. By now, it is misting rain again and the sky has darkened. Not a good night to be outdoors.

Lorene and I stand on the porch and watch the ambulance as it disappears into the night. "She'll be treated at Maury General," I say.

"We should go there now and talk to someone."

My phone rings and startles me. "Hello."

It's the All-State insurance agent calling me back.

"I need to take this call, Lorene. You go on to the hospital and I'll join you shortly." I go back in the house to get my coat and purse.

"I'm at your house, Ms. Powell. Can you come over?"

"Well, I'm kind of in a bind. Will it take long?" I reply, discounting the fact it is raining and dark outdoors. I need to get this done.

"Less than five minutes," Henry Clamper promises.

"Okay, but I can't stay longer than that."

"We won't need longer."

I lock up Lorene's house and hurry to my car. It's a short drive over to my house. A white van sits in the drive. It's too dark for me to read any writing on the side. I enter through the front door, since the backdoor has orange tape across it with a sign: DO NOT ENTER.

"Hello!" I call out.

The next thing I know, something falls over my head. At first, I think it's a spider web until I hear a voice I never wanted to hear again.

"Well, Ms. Powell, we meet again."

I peer through a veil of darkness and recognize the speaker.

"Mr. Hagen." My worst nightmare has just come true. "You can take off the blinders. I already saw your face," I declare with a boldness far superior to my usual demeanor. "Two years ago, I believe. How did you enjoy my sleeping cocktail? I hope your prison cell was as uncomfortable as I prayed it would be." I wonder what happens next.

Hagen laughs. "I told you she was a gas," he tells his partner.

I jerk off the head covering and view Henry Clamper for the first time. "I presume you do not work for All State." My eyes adjust to the darkness as the moon shines through the hole in my roof.

"You presume correctly," Hagen says. "Now, we are going to take a little drive." He looks at his partner-in-crime. "Jason, you can take off now. I won't need your assistance." He binds my hands behind my back and shoves me toward the foyer. "We're flying solo."

"Oh, I love the way you say solo since it's my preference, too."

He slaps me. "Shut up, Dorothy! I've had enough of your smart mouth. Five minutes with you makes me want to puke."

"Go ahead and shoot me! Make my day! Send me to Heaven so I can be with my husband—the one you murdered. Remember Arthur? I'm sure he's having quite a conversation with Jesus."

All my pompous words do not have any effect on the Mafia assassin. I think of how Clint—I mean Thomas—would handle this situation. He would keep the perpetrator talking and try to find out more about what is going on. Why I am targeted. Is this a kidnapping?

* * *

It's nine thirty and Dorothy has not arrived at Maury General Hospital. Claire is there and worried about her mother. Lorene says, "Dorothy's cell phone rang just as the EMS ambulance drove off."

"Any idea who called?"

Lorene shakes her head. "Your mother said she needed to take the call and would see me at the hospital shortly. I'm worried, too."

"That was two hours ago, Lorene."

"She's not answering her phone, either."

"Do you have any idea where she might be?" Claire asks.

"She's close to Clint Howard, maybe she's with him."

"Where does he live?" Claire asks.

"In that new apartment complex on E. Main Street. I don't know the number, but you could phone and ask the manager to check."

"Worth checking out." Claire Googles new apartment complexes in Columbia, Tennessee. The website appears as expected. She steps away to make the call. A few minutes later she reports to Lorene.

"There's no listing for Clint Howard," Claire says. "Beyond that, I could get no information out of the guy who answered the phone."

"That's odd." Lorene sees a doctor walking toward them.

Claire turns around. "Are you here to report on the condition of Alicia Anderton Colby?" she inquires. "We're her friends."

"Is there a family member present?" Dr. Weir asks.

"No, as far as we know Alicia has no living relatives."

"She's probably going to survive her injuries, but will need to be admitted to a care facility or live with someone who can take care of her." He looks for us to give him a decision. "One leg is broken."

"Can we get back to you on that?" Lorene inquires, thinking Alicia has the means to hire a full-time nurse if she stays in her log cabin.

"Sure, Miss Colby will be with us another few days."

"Thank you, Dr. Weir." Claire gives him her phone number.

Lorene intervenes and asks him to include her cell as a contact.

"Okay, ladies, it's late. You should both go home and get some rest," he suggests. "If there's any change, I'll see that you get a call."

Claire nods and takes Lorene by the arm. "Let's go."

They return to Lorene's house and she insists that Claire spend the night. If Dorothy is somewhere with Clint, she'll eventually call.

* * *

It's a two-hour drive east on I-40 before Mark Hagen exits on a county highway. After another twenty minutes, he drives the white van up a hilly gravel road and pulls into the driveway of a dilapidated farmhouse that appears vacant. The rolling hills have grown larger and the air much cooler due to the higher elevation. By my calculations, it's a property near Crossville, Tennessee. I wasn't blindfolded during the trip, and feel certain if Hagen intended harm, I would be dead by now.

"So, you have friends in low places here?" I ask as he turns off the motor and makes a phone call. "Shut up, woman!" is all I get back.

I sigh, praying that Lorene misses me and is talking to the police about searching for me. I hope Claire hasn't been told I'm out of pocket because I know it will worry her. Then, I've disappeared before and turned up uninjured. Maybe she's asleep and in a sweet dream.

* * *

"As long as my mother is missing, I can't sleep," Claire says to Lorene. It's 10:45 p.m. and they are seated in the den with the TV on low. An old cowboy flick is on the screen. "I could wring her neck."

Lorene groans. "I keep thinking of something Dorothy said."

"What's that?" Claire yawned.

"That she believes Clyde and Lorita Willems' deaths—or should I say murders—are connected to the Mafia," Lorene shares. "I believe I have a card with a phone number on it that Clint Howard dropped out of his pocket. He came here once—have I told you that?"

"No, Lorene. Can you put your hands on that card?" Claire asks. "Maybe whoever owns that number knows how to contact Clint. He seems to care for Mama, and we sure could use his help right now."

"I'll get it." Lorene goes to the kitchen and returns with the card. "Here. Call it," she says.

Claire punches in the number on the nameless card.

"Central Intelligence Agency, how may I assist you?"

Claire drops her cell phone. "It's the damn CIA!"

24

ELLIE AND LLOYD ARE seated in his Chevy Blazer after a quick meal at the Pizza Hut. It is after eleven p.m. "You never said what was discussed in your meeting with Stanley Kilpatrick." She was aware the FBI agent in charge was a busy man. Their topic of discussion must have been important. "Are we keeping secrets?"

"We?" He drew in his neck, a new growth of stubbly beard scratching his neck. "Ellie, I was told not to discuss the case."

"So, it was about the murder case. Lorita Willems?"

"Don't you ever give up?"

"No, and as I recall Kilpatrick thinks that's a good thing."

"If I tell you, can I come up to your apartment for a nightcap?" Lloyd bargained for a chance to get Ellie in bed. He was going crazy with her new rules. If only she'd move up the wedding date.

"As long as you understand it's one drink," she agrees.

They get out of the truck and Ellie leads the way to her apartment. "Did you talk to Dorothy Powell about purchasing her property?"

"No." He watches Ellie as she puts the key in the lock, except the door is already open. "Stay here." He pulls his weapon.

"I don't see anything missing or disturbed," he comes back and reports. "Are you sure you shut the door securely?"

"I may not have, I was in a hurry this morning," she replies.

"Where did you leave Pepper today?"

"I tried calling Dorothy and got no answer, so I took the little pup to the Vet's to keep for a few days." She looks at Lloyd. "Are we going to just stand here or go inside?" Her emerald eyes engage him.

"I want you to have the lock changed out tomorrow, Ellie," Lloyd says as he locates the bourbon bottle in the kitchen cabinet. "Drink?"

"No, thanks." Ellie yawns. "I don't want to be in a stupor tomorrow morning. I need to pay bills from last month."

Lloyd pours a double-shot and hurriedly drinks it.

"You shouldn't do that." Ellie lays her sweater on the arm of the sofa. "It's not healthy for your heart." She stands there, staring.

Feeling the impact of liquor, he walks over and pulls Ellie to him. "You know what I need, and it isn't alcohol." They kiss.

"I know, but there are rules." She pushes him away. "Tell me about your conversation with Kilpatrick."

"Are you going to be a nagging wife?"

"Of course, how else can I take proper care of you?"

He drops on the sofa, hands holding his dizzy head. Ellie is right. He's drinking too much lately. It will damage his liver. He feels Ellie's hand on his arm. "I can tell this case is eating at you, Lloyd."

He looks at her, eyes red from fatigue. "The blasted CIA planned Mark Hagen's escape from the federal prison," he admits.

"What?" Ellie cannot believe it. "Are they nuts?"

He scrubs his eyelids and tries to focus.

"Apparently, Clyde Willems left information about his Mafia associates. He saw the writing on the wall, they would kill him."

"What kind of information?" Ellie rubs Lloyd's arm.

"It's believed he's named Mafia bosses in several states," Lloyd reveals. "FBI learned about it from a snitch. So, they got Hagen out of prison, hoping he'd find the prize." Lloyd locks eyes with Ellie.

"They are nuts." Ellie twists her lips.

"Clint Howard is a CIA undercover agent sent to watch Dorothy Powell while Hagen is running loose," Lloyd adds as his phone rings.

"Who's calling this late?"

Lloyd stares at the I.D. caller. "Claire Burkes."

Ellie sits back, worried over everybody's safety.

"What can I do for you, Claire?" Lloyd inquires.

"Mama's missing, do you know anything about that?"

"No. Maybe she's off doing something stupid and decided not to tell you!" He slurs his words, not in any mood to talk with Claire.

"That is so like you, Butch," Claire fusses. "Do your damn job and find my mama, you hear me!"

Lloyd folds his phone in one hand.

"What was that call about?"

"Dorothy Powell is missing," he answers.

"Do you think Mark Hagen kidnapped her?" Ellie deducts. "The elderly woman could be stone-cold dead by now."

Lloyd nods. "I need to go back to the office."

"Want me to come with you?" Ellie asks.

"No, and lock up after I leave. This case is in the fast track now, and I have no idea where it will lead." He grabs his coat and leaves.

* * *

"It's cold in this house, are there any covers?" I ask from the dusty sofa, afraid to lie down at seeing roaches running about on the floor.

Mark doesn't answer, but continues to pace like a tiger.

"Did you squat at Lorene Perkin's house?"

"I stayed a few nights, why?"

"Just wondered."

He walks over and squats in front of me. "You want to live? Tell me where Clyde Willems hid the names of my friends."

"Your friends are criminals, why should I help you?" I yawn, wishing whoever is coming would get here and we could settle any dispute. I want to go home. If I don't, I'll surely go to Heaven.

25

Tuesday, November 8

"ARE YOU GOING TO VOTE today?" Dorothy asks Mark Hagen from a kitchen chair where her hands and feet are bound with packing tape.

"What are you talking about, old woman?" He's expecting a call from Leonard Stoldt, the Mafia boss presiding over Kentucky.

"Tennessee selects a new governor today, don't you care?"

"I won't be in Tennessee long enough to care!" he barks, so tired he just wants to pull the trigger and watch the pest bleed out.

"Is waiting for your call getting on your nerves?"

"Shut up, or I'll permanently end all conversations!" he threatens.

I laugh at him. "I think you have bigger fish in charge of whatever is going on here." Inside I shake with fear staring into his devilish eyes.

"Do you even know there's a Black List?"

He stands over me with his fists knotted in preparation to strike.

"Don't kid yourself, Mark, I stay current with affairs."

"And just what does that mean?"

I know what a Black List is because I watch a popular series by that name. The bad guys always lose. "We should have some coffee. It might settle your nerves a bit, and I need some caffeine."

"I don't think you care if you die."

"Why should I? Christians know where they're going in the Afterlife," I tell him. "You'll never step one foot in Heaven, boy. Still, I can't help feeling sorry for you. God's judgment won't be pretty."

"What do you know about judgment, old woman?"

"I read the Bible. I know enough. How many murder scalps have you collected over the years? I bet God is not pleased with you."

He backhands my left cheek and I can't help for crying out. Still, I say, "Thank you, Mark. Every strike is a crown on my head."

So angry, he could spit nails, yet he steps away from the foolish woman and paces the room. Finally, the phone rings.

"Yeah?" Mark grabs his burner phone.

I listen carefully to the one-sided conversation and learn nothing.

"What did your boss say?" I ask when the call ends.

"Your newest best friend has the code."

He's talking about Clint Howard. Does he know he's CIA?

"Aw, so you know that Clyde Willems left the coded names of your criminal associates." I pray he doesn't have the list tucked away in the children's book. "You're too late. By now, the feds have all the information needed to arrest your buddies. Maybe you should run."

Mark leans against a wall, just glaring at me. His not saying anything is even scarier. "Penny for your thoughts?"

* * *

Joe Wilson Jr. corners Thomas in the kitchen and says, "Dorothy Powell has been abducted. Jack thinks Hagen has her again."

Again, refers to when the Mafia assassin kidnapped Dorothy from her home two years ago and she fed him sleeping pills to escape.

"I've been told to stay out of the case," Tom says as he fills a mug with black coffee. That he cares for Dorothy deepens his concern.

"Just giving you a heads up," Joe pipes. "I don't think her life matters much to the CIA; it's all about capturing the Mafia bosses."

Tom inhales deeply. *He's right.* Dorothy doesn't deserve to be murdered because the CIA has failed to keep up with Hagen.

No, I may get fired, but I'm going back to help her.

Thirty minutes later, Tom tells the Director he's going home to pack for his international trip and take care of some monthly bills. He does exactly that, then takes an American flight out of D.C. at noon due to arrive in Nashville at 3:32 p.m. Claire Burkes will pick him up.

The plane lands on time and Tom exits the airport.

"Thanks for coming back," Claire says as Tom slips into the passenger seat of her shiny Buick.

"I owe her that, at least." He buckles his seatbelt.

"You broke my mama's heart." Claire drives too fast out of the airport. "She's a big girl, why didn't you just ask for her help?"

Tom massages the tight muscles in his neck. He didn't get much sleep last night. "My real name is Thomas Kessler. Call me Tom."

"I know, you're CIA."

"Smart, like your mother." He shrugs.

"Where are we going, Tom?" Claire's voice is as cold as ice.

He checks the weather on his cell phone. "Looks like Nashville is in for an ice storm. The interstate could get dicey."

"Well, that's apropos since Mama caught the killer during a snowstorm," Claire recalls. "Where do you think she is?"

"According to our snitch, there's a house not far from Crossville that the Mafia uses on occasions. Feel like a little drive?"

"Never better." Claire puts her foot to the pedal.

* * *

Lorene stands by the bed that holds the frail ninety-two-year-old Alicia Anderton Colby. "I'm so glad you woke up," she tells her. "You had us all scared to death when you fell down my staircase."

Alicia bats her weak eyes. Her wrinkled face is bruised and her left leg is in a cast from the knee down. She's on strong pain meds.

"Where is Dorothy?" Alicia struggles to sit up.

"Don't." Lorene warns. "We don't know. Claire is working on finding her." She's learned Clint Howard is coming back to help.

"I wish I could do something," Alicia says in a very British brogue. "Dorothy's a sweetheart. I hope nothing bad has happened to her."

"God is good, He's watching over her," Lorene replies, praying that is true. Dorothy also has the Luck of the Irish, so maybe . . .

* * *

"I have to pee," I tell Mark. "I'm too old to run so untie me and I'll take care of my personal business then fix us some grub."

He glares at her. "I don't understand why you aren't scared."

"Faith, dear boy. I don't depend on normal circumstances, you see. God has a way of changing all of that for a Christian's benefit."

He groans, not feeling like listening to another sermon from the foolish old woman who will bite a bullet before the day is over.

But not until Leonard talks to her first.

26

"ARE YOU GOING TO tell me what is going on?" Claire asks CIA operative Thomas Kessler as darkness wraps its tight arms around them and ice pebbles tumble down the Buick's windshield.

Tom had insisted on driving as she rides shotgun, wondering what lies in front of them when they locate her mother. "Tell me, Tom."

He heaves a sigh. "I owe you that."

"Yes, you do. What has Mama gotten herself into?"

"None of this is your mother's fault," he says, glancing in the rearview mirror to assess if anyone is tailing them.

"Something tells me she welcomes trouble." Claire stared into the dimly lit road, troubled over the danger, though Tom seems capable.

"Dorothy is a natural at detective work." He switches on the radio and seeks a station reporting the current weather conditions.

"I just don't understand why you've put Mama in the middle of an investigation that's none of her business." Claire studies him.

"We—the CIA—knew that once Mark Hagen had broken out of prison he'd come for your mother. She took him down two years ago, and now he wants to return the favor. But, there's something more important to him than revenge. That is why we involved Dorothy."

Claire's blue eyes enlarge, "So, tell me. Help me understand."

Tom passed a stalled truck parked on the side of the interstate.

"It is believed that Clyde Willems has been associated with the Russian Mafia for many decades. He's gambled, borrowed money, then paid his debts to the bosses in various ways. His illegal activities caught up with him. He knew about the prostitution ring in Nashville."

"And the Mafia didn't trust him to be discreet."

"No trust among thieves. Clyde saw Death in his near future."

"What about the money he borrowed from my daddy?"

"The ten thousand dollars? I doubt it was ever enough to pay off his gambling debts." Tom braked the car and slowed down.

"Are you sure the interstate is safe to drive on?"

"We have no choice. I need to find the safehouse where Hagen is likely keeping Dorothy. He needs something from her," Tom reveals.

"What could an assassin possibly need from my mother?"

"Information. Dorothy and I located a book Clyde gave your daddy on his last birthday before he was murdered," Tom reveals.

"Mama never said anything to me about a book."

"She didn't realize its importance until recently. It's a children's book. *The Secret Garden.*" He glances at Claire, beautiful like her mother.

"Him giving Daddy that doesn't make any sense."

"Exactly." Claire will figure it out soon.

"But *you* have a good idea, don't you?"

"Okay, you win. The book contained secrets. Possibly the names of Clyde's Mafia associates. The Russians are international in their prostitute activities. Our sting was coordinated with the TBI."

"The CIA needed Hagen free?"

"Yep."

"Free to look for the secrets Clyde horded," Claire concluded.

"At first it was thought the information was hidden in the log cabin, but a thorough search revealed nothing," Tom explains.

"Were some of your associates Alicia Colby's prowlers?"

"Lots of tracks out there in the woods," he replies. "Some are ours; some are theirs." He refers to the CIA versus the Russian Mafia.

"Seems to me you guys were looking for a needle in a haystack."

"In a way, we were. We needed a break-through."

"Well, that didn't work out so well!" Claire exclaims.

"A snitch who gambled with Clyde told one of our undercover agents that Clyde bragged he had the goods on the Russian Mafia."

"And naturally the information got back to Mark Hagen."

"No, actually, we did that. We arranged his escape from prison."

"Son of a gun!" Claire restrained from cussing. "You let that lunatic loose knowing he would come after my mother?"

"That's why I moved to Columbia, to keep her safe."

"And in the meantime, you broke her heart."

"Well, it was kind of a two-way street," he said, reaching for his billfold and handing it to Claire. "Look at the photographs."

Claire opened the billfold. "You have my mother's picture."

He smiles. "No, that picture was taken twenty years ago. Angela, and my son, a month before Mark Hagen murdered them."

"She looks just like my mother. Did you know?"

"Yes, but I didn't tell anyone, or I would not have been assigned to protect her," he admits. "I really respect your mother."

Claire nods, teary-eyed and staring out the icy windshield. "I need to potty. Get off the next exit, I also need a cup of strong coffee."

"Sure, in fact the next exit is for Crossville."

"What if my mother is not there?"

"Then we've wasted a trip."

Claire chewed on that thought and felt nauseous.

Tom reached over and grasped her hand.

"If you're going to tell me everything will work out for the best," forget it, Agent Kessler. "My mother's life is on the line."

27

SAC STANLEY KIRKPATRICK HEADS up a team of TBI agents as they approach Columbia, Tennessee in a Bell Jet Ranger helicopter. It's only on the ground long enough to take on one passenger, Detective Lloyd Peters. It's believed that the assassin Mark Hagen has kidnapped Dorothy Powell and she is being held captive at a known safehouse for the Russian Mafia located near Crossville, Tennessee.

"Buckle up, Detective, it's going to be a bumpy ride," Stan says.

With the rotors so loud, Lloyd can hardly think; he simply nods to Kilpatrick, takes his seat among the others, then buckles up.

None of the four guys and two female agents look happy.

The pilot lifts off the tarmac and heads east as a treacherous weather front moves in from the northwest. Ten inches of snow is predicted for the East Tennessee Appalachian Mountain range, Crossville's elevation earning the countryside their fair share of fluff.

* * *

A four-wheel-drive suburban pulls up in front of the dilapidated farmhouse as Mark Hagen stares out the window at the bleak night.

"Boss is finally here," he mutters to Dorothy, strapped in a straight chair with packing tape. "I hope you've come to your senses."

"Whoopee! Nice to have a visitor beside you." She spits at him.

The saliva runs down her neck and it turns as cold as the house, heated only by the glowing flames struggling from the fireplace. At least Mark had the decency to collect wood and start a warm fire.

The door comes open and Leonard Stoldt tromps in, his rubber boots covered in sloshy mud and remnants of snow. He's Italian by birth but was raised in Russia by an aunt on his mother's side.

The Mafia boss is small, five-foot-six maybe, and weighs less than one-hundred-thirty pounds. He has a manicured mustache the color of charcoal and hardened beady eyes to match. He reminds Dorothy of a porcupine since he has a widow's peak and his glossy coarse black hair is a straight comb-back. He stares at me like I'm his prey.

"Good evening, Mr. Stoldt," I say. "Sorry the weather is so awful. Did you have a difficult time getting here? Mark was quite anxious."

"Funny girl." He locks cold eyes on Mark.

117

"She hasn't told me anything," he informs Stoldt.

"You said she was a hard ass, so I would expect no less."

Stoldt takes off his leather gloves and heavy coat. He stamps his boots on the roughhewn wooded floor and approaches the fireplace.

"Fire feels good, do you have coffee made?"

"Dorothy made some not long ago," Mark replies.

"Well, well, a domestic female!" Stoldt comments. "Untie her, I'm hungry. Are there fresh eggs in the refrigerator and decent bread?"

"Yes, sir," Mark respectively replies. "Dana stocked the kitchen early this morning. We got here just after dark," he reveals.

I shake out my tingling hands as the tape is ripped off. My skin is chaffed and stings. "Do you prefer fried or scrambled eggs?" I ask. "I'm pretty good at stirring up an omelet if there's cheese on location."

Stoldt appears surprised. "Is she always this accommodating?"

"Sure, a chameleon that changes colors with the environment."

I smile at his description of me.

"Beware, give her a chance and she'll strike like a snake. You won't know what hit you until the poison takes you down!" Mark barks.

He's still mad at me for giving him sleeping pills.

"I heard she was the one that captured you two years ago." Stoldt's upturned palms are close to the leaping flames in the hearth.

"Shall I make breakfast now?" I ask, biding my time. *Keep them talking.* Help will surely come, I tell myself. *Have a little faith.*

I think of what Clint, I mean Tom, said to me.

* * *

The Jet Bell helicopter lands at a small airport in Crossville, Tennessee, and the crew aboard dismounts and crawls into two black SUVs with shaded windows. Their headlights are bright beams cutting through the blizzard assaulting the town. And it's freezing outdoors.

Lloyd has said little since they left Columbia. He's concerned that Dorothy may somehow be killed in an unavoidable skirmish. Mark Hagen and whoever else is with him will not easily be apprehended.

GPS tells the two drivers how to get to the safehouse.

The county roads are slick, and several times wheels have skidded off the road and the vehicles have nearly wrecked. But the drivers are experts and manage to plow through the accumulating snow with skill.

SUV lights went off a good mile from the house. No moonlight tonight makes it even more difficult to stay on the last trek of gravel road. Finally, the drivers kill the engines and everyone piles out.

They walk to the house under the cloak of darkness.

Fortunately, glowing windows at the property give the agents a point of reference, like walking toward Glory, only they will likely encounter Hell when they arrive. Lloyd prepares for conflict.

* * *

"The scrambled eggs with cheese and onion were excellent, Mrs. Powell," Leonard Stoldt compliments me. "I would hire you as my cook, if we were not on opposite sides of the law."

Mark sits in a rocking chair, chuckling over Stoldt's remark.

"I enjoy cooking, Mr. Stoldt," I tell him. "My husband liked to eat." I've used the past tense since the Mafia murdered him.

"Arthur Powell," Stoldt says. "Yes, a shame he got in the way."

"People have choices, Mr. Stoldt."

"Be prepared for a dose of poison tea," Mark hawks.

I suddenly realize Mark was the person who murdered Lorita Willems. Why else would he make reference to poison tea? He could not risk Lorita exposing the Mafia leadership, though she'd kept quiet for two years. I have solved the crime and strangely feel emboldened.

"Have a seat, Dorothy. I have a few questions for you," Stoldt points to a dusty sofa. "You're an old woman, cooperate and I may decide to let you live. I think your culinary skills are worth saving."

"Why, thank you, Leonard." I try to smile as I sit down. A puff of dust rises from the sofa and I sneeze. "Sorry." I sneeze again.

Stoldt grabs a straight chair from the kitchen table and drags it across the plank floors. The scraping is annoying as I stare at him.

"Now . . ." he sits backwards in the chair, his stone-cold black eyes staring at me. "Tell me about the treasure Clyde Willems horded."

"Well, how far back do you want me to go?"

I am doing my darndest to keep him talking until help arrives.

"First, tell me about Clint Howard. Why did he let you go?"

I am taken back by his question. "He likes me," I say.

Mark snickers from his rocking chair.

"And why does he like you?" Stoldt plays along, amused.

"He says I look like his wife."

"Really?" Mark sits up straight.

"Really," I say back.

"He called and said he was sick, is that true?"

"I don't know, I haven't spoken with him since last Friday." It's the truth and I'm worried he might have gotten Covid-19. And that nasty Delta version is out there, too. *Oh, Tom, please don't die.*

"Mark, come here," Stoldt orders, his forefinger hooking.

"Yes, sir?"

"What were you told in prison about a list of names Clyde hid?"

"Supposedly, the names of four Mafia bosses were written down—yours included," he tells Stoldt. "He probably intended to use it as an insurance policy, so he'd live a few more years."

"But, of course, you couldn't wait," Stoldt says.

I get the sense the Mafia boss is not thrilled with Mark's showmanship. He might actually be in as much danger as I am.

"We looked all over Clyde's log cabin and found nothing," Mark reports as he idly stands, waiting for further instructions.

"That's because the evidence was buried in his garden," I reveal.

Four pairs of eyes turn on me. "Do the feds have the names?"

I quirk my head to one side. "I don't know, and that's the truth." *Keep them talking, this is going pretty well so far.*

Mark slurs, "She's useless, shoot her!"

He's been drinking, and it wasn't coffee.

Stoldt holds up a hand, not having moved from the chair.

"What else can you tell us, Dorothy?"

I think a moment, needing a clever response. "All I can say is everything you see with your eyes, or think you know, may not be as it really is." I'm referring to Clint as an undercover CIA agent.

Stoldt burst out laughing. "I like this lady, she's clever."

"As a viper!" Mark curses and limps back to his corner. It's not a fair fight and I know it. I am at a big disadvantage, one elderly woman against two younger hardened criminals evading the law.

"Let's try another approach," Stoldt says. "If you were to venture a guess, where would you hide the evidence?"

"In plain sight," I recall a movie I once viewed.

The violence on Mark's face says he's close to pulling a gun and aiming it at me. I don't know much, except his patience will run out.

28

LLOYD CREEPS AROUND THE safehouse to the backdoor. TBI Agent James is at his side, a listening device plugged into one ear as he awaits orders. Kirkpatrick is at the front door with the two female agents and a huge bodyguard his teammates dubbed "Desperado."

The signal is given and all Hell breaks loose and cabin doors are knocked down and windows explode from the side of the house.

Tom and Claire observe the explosion as they reach the end of the driveway to the house. If Dorothy is inside, she's in serious danger.

* * *

The firepower is deafening. I leap from my chair and crawl behind the sofa as bullets whiz overhead. Lights are off, electricity crashed, or unplugged by our assailants. I cover my ears and pray it's the TBI or CIA. Dare I hope that Tom is coming to save me? *God, help me!*

Furniture breaking, feet scuffling, hand-to-hand combat in process, I know of nothing I can do but stay hidden and wait for it all to end. One opponent will win. Either the good guys or the bad.

Finally, the firing stops. The cabin is cloaked in stillness. I slowly rise and see Mark Hagen pointing a pistol at me. He's wounded, on the floor bleeding out. But I know he wants me to die with him.

I cover my face and wait to see Arthur. I hope he gets me with one bullet and I don't have to suffer pain as Death collects me for eternity. Then, Jesus will tell the Father I am one of his followers.

O Death! Where is your sting!

I hear the gunshot but I feel nothing. Then the weight of someone falls on me. A flashlight shines in my face. "Are you all right, Dorothy?" Detective Lloyd Peters asks. "Sorry about your friend."

I shove the weight off me and sit up. Thomas Kessler stares at me, blood oozing out his stomach. "Help him!" I cry out.

Then Claire kneels beside me. I hear the bleating sirens of ambulances coming closer. "Help Tom, Claire! I'm fine."

"Mark Hagen and his buddy are dead, Mama."

My head throbs and I'm not thinking straight. "How did you get here, Claire?" I ask. "Did Tom bring you?"

"Yes." She stands aside as the emergency medical team attends to Tom and straps him on a stretcher. I move out of their way.

The houselights come on and I see blood splattered on the walls. This house needs to be burnt to the ground. I am suddenly aware of how cold I feel. Air and snow rush through broken windowpanes.

"Let's get out of here, Mama," Claire says.

She walks me to her Buick and we stand there in a blizzard watching Thomas Kessler ride away in an ambulance.

"Will I ever see him again?" I ask myself more than Claire.

"I doubt it, he's undercover, Mama."

I hug my daughter. "I love you, honey."

"I love you, too, Mama."

29

Wednesday, November 9

CLAIRE'S PHYSICIAN EXAMINED ME earlier today. I was dehydrated but my vital signs and bloodwork were satisfactory. Above all else, I was worried that Tom had not survived his stomach wound. He'd taken Mark Hagen's bullet to save my life, a sacrificial act of love that was second none to Jesus Christ who gave me eternal life.

It was clear to me his love was genuine. And I'd probably never have the chance to tell him I returned his feelings. Yet, in my heart of hearts, I knew a relationship with him would set us both up for greater heartache. I'm sorry his wife Angela died, but I'm not her.

"What are you doing, Mama?"

Claire stands in the doorway to her guest bedroom with a mug of coffee in hand. "Surely, you're not contemplating going home."

"Lorene phoned. Alicia is scheduled to be released from Maury General Hospital later this afternoon and she needs my assistance."

"An ambulance can take her home," Claire points out.

"Who will take care of her when she gets there?" I lock eyes with my beautiful daughter and wish I were thirty years younger. We have the same color blue eyes, but her complexion is still youthful and flawless while more wrinkles attack my face every new day.

"Besides," I add, "Jeff Pauley phoned to say he's received an estimate on the repairs my house requires and wants to meet."

"The All-State Insurance agent," Claire nods, "I'll call Ted and tell him I'm driving you home." She approaches and hugs me.

"That won't be necessary; Butch is coming for me."

"Lloyd Peters, why?"

"He wants to pick my brain, so he can finish his report regarding the murder of Lorita Willems. I need to tell him who killed her."

Claire crosses her arms, leans against the doorjamb and snickers.

"Mama, you act like you're a bonified detective."

"I don't need a sheet of paper to prove I have skills."

Claire throws up her hands. "What time is he coming?"

"Now." I hear a horn blasting from Claire's driveway. "That will be Butch." He's no gentleman, but I don't care. I need a ride home.

Claire waves as I open the passenger door to his antiquated Chevy Blazer. I hope when he's married Ellie, he will purchase a classier ride. She's several paygrades above him and deserves more.

"Good afternoon, Ms. Powell." He backs out of the driveway.

"Are we really going to do this, Butch." I buckle up. "Just call me Dorothy and I'll be nice and refer to you as Lloyd. Deal?"

"Deal." He chuckles, says, "So, I understand you had quite an adventure Monday evening. I'd like to hear about what happened."

"Are you going to tape me, because I'm only going to say this once," I inform him as he holds up his phone. "It's recording?"

He nods. "How did you get yourself in this situation?"

"Well," he exits Claire's expensive neighborhood and hooks a left as he heads for I-65 South, "you're aware that Clint Howard was working undercover for the CIA. Thomas was respectful of me."

Butch threw a hand. "I know all that. When did the trouble start?"

"Lorene Perkins and I were about to follow the ambulance to the hospital—Alicia Colby had fallen down her stairs and needed medical assistance. Turns out she broke her leg," I add.

"Just the facts ma'am," Butch says as he ramps onto the interstate. "Tell me about when Mark Hagen abducted you."

I stare out the window at the sunny day. The snow is melting on the bright landscape, and it's thirty degrees warmer. "I received a call from a man named Henry Clamper just before we left Lorene's house."

"To follow the ambulance carrying Miss Colby," he clarifies.

"Yes, Henry said my regular All-State agent had a family emergency and he had the repair estimates for my damaged property. He said he was at my house and wanted me to come over." I pause to reflect upon that moment. "I told Lorene I'd meet her at the hospital after I ran an errand." I pause. "Only I never got the chance."

"Hagen was waiting for you at the house." Butch's cat-like eyes are on the pavement unspooling in front of us as he passes a car.

"Yes, then drove me to the Mafia's safehouse near Crossville, Tennessee," I report. "Leonard Stoldt arrived later that night."

"I'm aware of what happened after the TBI stormed the house and saved you," Butch says. "Did you tell Stoldt anything important?"

I glance over at him. "I don't know anything important. The last time I saw Agent Thomas Kessler, he was taking *The Secret Garden* to an expert concerning World War II German spy tactics."

"Now, that is news to me," Butch says with satisfaction.

"Clyde Willems gave Arthur a birthday gift in August, two months before Mark Hagen murdered him. I later found the children's book and donated it to the library. So, Clint—that was the name he went by—accompanied me to the library and we asked Lucy Panetta for a list of my donated books." I pause. "We finally located the title."

"Why was that book important?"

"I can't believe the CIA, or TBI, has not read you in on these important details," I say. "Are they going to try and shut me up?"

Butch chuckles. "I don't think you are in any danger, Dorothy."

"Anyhow . . ." I gather my thoughts, "Clint and I found words circled on the pages. A number of words. We wondered if Clyde was giving Arthur information regarding the Russian Mafia network."

"Now, that I've heard about," Lloyd says.

"I was never read into what secrets the book revealed."

"So, you have no idea what information Clyde was hording." He mulls over the situation. "Did Hagen or Stoldt hurt you?"

"No, I kept them talking—oh, but I learned an important fact from Mark Hagen when he warned Mr. Stoldt that I was dangerous and might slip him a cup of poison tea." I study Butch's response.

He blinks and pounds the steering wheel. "You deduct that Hagen provided the poison tea Lorita Willems ingested."

I smile. "It makes perfect sense, right? The CIA arranges for the assassin to escape the federal prison. Mark believes Lorita knows where Clyde hid the information that would damage the Mafia." I am on a roll to complete Butch's report and get on with my own sad life.

He cuts off the camera with a recording device and folds the phone in one hand. "Yes, it does, Dorothy. Where shall I take you?"

"Lorene Perkin's house, she's waiting for me."

30

BY 5:30 P.M. LORENE AND I deliver Alicia Colby to her log cabin. Lorene had arranged for a cleaning service to come on Tuesday. Her two sons had also raked the dead grass and trimmed the shrubs. Lorene's attention to the property was rewarded by Alicia's big smile.

"I don't know what I would have done without you girls."

Lorene tells Alicia it was her privilege and was sure Alicia would have done the same for her. We go out the backdoor and peer at the messy yard. The Mafia and TBI boys have left huge holes while digging for Clyde's critical evidence against the Russian Mafia.

"Don't worry, Alicia, my boys and I will fix this," Lorene says.

"You have gone beyond friendship, both of you."

I love Alicia's British accent. She is God's precious creation. If I hang around her long enough, maybe I'll pick up some of her brogue.

Alicia uses a crutch as she hobbles back inside the cabin.

"I'm in the mood for some hot tea." She looks at us both.

"Sure, let me help you," I say as I walk into the kitchen and fill the tea kettle with tap water. Alicia and Lorene sit at the small table in the corner by a picture window. "My yard looks so nice, I can't wait to plant a garden out back when spring arrives," Alicia tells Lorene as she enthusiastically raps her crutch twice on the floor and chuckles.

I wait for the water to boil in the kettle and set off the whistle.

We sit together enjoying the Lancashire Tea Lorene and I purchased for Alicia as a house-warming gift. No poison, thankfully.

"I thought I'd stay the night with you," I tell Alicia.

"Well, I only have one bedroom, Dorothy."

"And I suppose you'd like to sleep comfortably," I add.

"She kicks off the covers," Lorene attests to the facts.

"Really, I have the prepaid phone you purchased for me," Alicia says. "I will be just fine. You both need to go home."

I snicker. "Did you forget I don't have a home?"

"You have mine," Lorene says.

"Oh, I forgot to call my All-State agent," I report and look for a signal on my cell phone. The landline rings. "Is Mr. Pauley there?"

I hear the phone click on a hard surface as I wait.

"This is Jeff Pauley."

"Mr. Pauley, this is Dorothy Powell. When can we get together?"

"Come to my office at ten a.m. tomorrow morning."

"It's a date." I end the call.

"So, you're coming home with me," Lorene says.

"Yes, but I don't want a thousand questions that will prevent me from having a restful night, are we in agreement?" I bargain.

"As long as I hear your story sometime tomorrow."

"Sure." I'm thinking of writing a book.

* * *

Lloyd and Ellie are seated in a bar drinking beers. He'd worked late at the office completing his report. He'd used Dorothy Powell's conclusions to the murder case and considered it closed. Lorita Willems was a decent hardworking person and didn't deserve to die.

Ellie yawns. "I think it's time for you to take me home."

"Are you going to let me spend the night?"

"Of course not, Butch. Rules have consequences."

He shrugs and mutters, "They sure do."

She reaches across the table and grasps Lloyd's sweaty hand. "I spoke to my mother early this afternoon. She's arranged with a Four-Star Hotel in Chicago to host our reception. We are to be married in the First United Presbyterian Church in the heart of the city."

"How many people are invited?" Lloyd inwardly groaned.

"I told her to keep it down to fifty."

"Who's paying for our shindig?" He still wanted to elope.

"My parents, so please don't let the expense concern you," Ellie says. "My grandparents owned land around Chicago so the sky's the limit as far as my parents are concerned. And I want a nice wedding."

He groans. "This isn't your first ceremony, Ellie."

"Because I'm not wearing white, I don't deserve the best?"

"I never said that." He holds both of her hands. "I just hate big weddings. All I want is you. Forget about all the hoopla."

Tears are in her eyes. "I love you for saying that."

Lloyd bows his head, thinking he's ruined everything.

"Rules are to be broken," Ellie says. "Come home with me. I think I know how to lift your mood." She stands up. "I love you."

Suddenly, the night has just brightened.

31

Friday, November 11

THE CONTRACTOR AND HIS crew are at my house doing the repairs as Lorene and I enter the Senior Citizens Center. I am reminded of the first day I brought Alicia Colby here for lunch and met Clint Howard for the first time. That seems like a lifetime ago, yet it has only been a few weeks. My perspective of how my life should unfold has changed.

I am not the same person since I met Tom. He's somehow made me stronger, forcing me to think of a future when I thought I had nothing to look forward to but my headstone in a graveyard. Though, Claire would probably opt to cremate me and toss me to the wind.

I giggle. That would get me out of her hair permanently.

"What's so funny?" Lorene asks as we search for a vacant seat at a table. Lunch has already been served. We are late because I insisted on stopping by my house first to make sure the carpenters were at work. I no longer trust people to do what they say. I smile again.

"I swear, Dorothy, you are in some kind of mood today."

"Well, Lorene," I look at her, "if you'd been through what I have in the past few weeks you'd be in a mood, too."

"Okay, okay . . ." she waved a hand. "Truce."

"We were never fighting." I look around and see a man about my age with a headful of thick gray hair coming toward us.

Lorene notices my staring. "That's the new manager."

"How old is he?" I inquire.

"Over sixty-five," she answers while giggling. "He has a wife." She points at a fine-looking female two tables over. "Gloria Bolton."

I squint my eyes to focus better. "She looks familiar."

"She should, Dorothy. Miss Columbia High of 1960. Miss Tennessee in 1966. Formerly Cynthia Ann Lake, born and bred in this historic town," Lorene reveals. "She dated Arthur before you did."

Double D-D! "I already don't like her more than I used to."

Lorene elbows me in the side. "Don't tell Gerry I said that. He's on his way over here to greet you." We both notice he is limping.

He stands six feet tall, with dark eyes and graying eyebrows. He looks familiar, too. "Gerry Bolton," I recall he graduated three years after I did. That would make him seventy-nine. "How are you?"

"Dorothy Powell, I'd recognize you anywhere." Gerry pulls me to my feet and plants a wet kiss on my cheek. "It's so good to see you."

"It's good to see you, too, Gerry."

Lorene sits quietly watching.

"I was so sorry to hear about Arthur's passing. You may recall we played together on the newly organized soccer team, the Skyhawks."

Embarrassed, I sit back down. "I see you married Gloria Lake. What was it, her third try at relationships?" That was ugly. My bad.

"Now, Dorothy, you haven't changed a bit. You and Gloria are a mismatch made in Heaven," he teases. "We've been married five years. Her second husband died of Alzheimer's." He holds to his cane.

"Did you receive an injury?" I ask as he continues to stand.

"Yes, skiing, ten years ago. My first wife, Mary, thought we would live forever and continue to do all the things we did as teens."

"Did Mary pass?" I ask.

"Right into the arms of a younger, more handsome man."

My face is beet-red. I feel perspiration soaking my underarms.

"Well, it looks like you did alright for yourself, Gerry. I'm sure Gloria provides plenty of entertainment and exercise for you both."

He smiles. "Same old Dorothy."

"Why don't you bring Gloria by my house one day soon," Lorene intervenes, seeing the topic of sexual compatibility has come up.

"We'll do that, Lorene. I'll have Gloria give you a call about a time." He looks down at me. "Great seeing you, Dorothy."

"You, too." I smile back, not missing the fact Gloria is staring at us. If looks were knives, I'd have one right through my heart.

Lunch is burgers with all the trimmings and sodas. We select the kind of packaged chips we want and move through the serving line.

At one o'clock, the crowd disburses, some going home and others preparing to play games for the afternoon. Of course, Lorene, Lizzy, Jane Murphy, and I sit down at a card table to play Canasta. We've done this every Friday for twenty years. Lorene has always been my best friend, though Lizzy has done her best to squeeze into our small circle. I still barely know Jane. She's usually so quiet and reserved.

Which makes me think of Tom. I pray he survived his wounds.

"Why the sad face, Dorothy?" Jane asks.

I am surprised by her question. "I'm not sad."

"I heard Mr. Howard took a bullet to save you," she says.

"Where did you hear that?" I query, worried there is more gossip floating around town about my personal relationship with Tom.

"The grapevine still works well," Lizzy hones in.

I bite my lip, not knowing what to say.

"Lay off, girls," Lorene defends me. "When Dorothy is ready to share her clandestine experience with us, she will."

I blink. How does Lorene know it's *clandestine*?

"Cat got your tongue," Jane says and I perceive she is angry with me. We draw cards to see who will deal. Lizzy wins.

"Have I done something to offend you, Jane?" I ask.

She frowns and doesn't answer.

"Okay, girls, what in the world is going on?" I ask, thinking I've missed something huge sitting right in front of me.

"I take it you have not read the latest issue of the *Tennessean*," Lizzy remarks. "There's an article in there about the CIA operation."

My heart drops in my chest. I grab my stomach like it's going all the way through me and slamming my guts on the floor.

"What does that have to do with me?" I inquire.

Lizzy locks eyes with Jane then says, "An unnamed woman is mentioned in the article. Apparently, she was instrumental in providing information that led to the arrests of four Mafia bosses."

"And you think I'm that woman?"

"We know you are, Dorothy." Jane smirks. "My grandson is an EMT, and his best friend drove the ambulance that took Mr. Howard to the hospital. Bill saw you there at the house. Don't deny it."

My mouth is powder-dry. I need to give them something. Certainly, not intimate facts about my relationship with Tom.

"Just tell us!" Lorene demands.

"It's not like you think, girls," I say. "Detective Peters started this mess when he asked me to spy on Alicia Colby. I was targeted by the CIA from the get-go so they could identify and arrest some bad guys."

The deck of cards lay on the table between us while I explained why Clint Howard came to town and why he paid so much attention to me—leaving out the fact I looked like his deceased wife Angela.

"It was believed Clyde Willems left evidence with Arthur that would name people involved with the Russian Mafia. It turned out to be true." That was all I intended to say on the disturbing subject.

"So, Clint leaped in front of you to keep an assassin from killing you because that was his job?" Lizzy appeared disappointed. "We were hoping for a more romantic ending. That jerk!"

I laugh. "You thought Clint and I were a couple?"

Jane, sniffling, said, "Appearances mean something, Dorothy."

"He was undercover, Jane. He was hired to protect me."

"Well . . ." Lizzy deals the cards, "I still think you should write a book." We each gather and organize our thirteen cards in hand.

I have four aces and think that must mean something in a universal kind of way. Maybe, Thomas Kessler and I will meet again.

32

Thursday, November 24

MY GREAT-GRANDDAUGHTER JUNE recovered from Covid with no side effects, at least none that were noticeable. Claire insisted we celebrate Thanksgiving at her house this year, and I did not contest the choice. I had not seen Tom again and missed him terribly. I did not even know if he had survived the bullet Mark Hagen fired at me.

"Penny for your thoughts, Mama."

"Goodness! Everybody wants to pick my brain these days!"

We are in the kitchen finishing up the holiday meal. It's a nice day outdoors with no rain or snow forecast. My contribution to dinner is two pecan pies because I know how much Ted likes the dessert.

Claire whips the baked sweet potatoes then adds brown sugar and cinnamon to sweeten the dish. I watch as she pours the concoction in a long baking dish and shoves it in the oven on 350 degrees Fahrenheit.

"I don't mean to pry, Mama, but you seem sad."

I rinse my hands in the kitchen sink and dry them with a towel.

"I'm not exactly sad, just trying to get past what's happened to me in the last month. I've been homeless and used by a federal agency to promote a cause they never told me about. I feel somewhat abused."

"But getting to know Tom was worth it, right?"

My daughter is very perceptive. "Maybe I should have taken Mark Hagen's bullet; he's still a young man," I tell her forthright.

"You feel guilty because Tom did his job?"

I nod, a tear slipping down one cheek.

"Mama, he showed me the picture of his deceased wife and son," Claire reveals for the first time. "He really cared about you."

I nod, praying that is so. He was undercover, and I know agents lie when it favors their purposes. I'm not stupid. "I hope so."

An hour later, Claire removes the sweet potato casserole from the oven and puts the fourteen-pound turkey injected with Cajun seasoning in to bake for four hours. Dinner will be served at five p.m.

Patrick and Helen and their two children will be here by four, and Benjamin is bringing a girl we hope he will marry. It will be a family affair. So, Arthur's seat will remain vacant for yet another year.

* * *

Lorene Perkins stands on the front porch as her son Graham assists Alicia Colby as she crawls out the back door of his Toyota. He's still a handsome man at forty-five and loves working as a pharmacist at Walgreen's. Dr. Cynthia Preston, the Medical Examiner for Maury County, exits the passenger seat and waves at her prospective mother-in-law. She's been engaged to Graham for a month. Joyfully.

"Come in, all of you!" Lorene calls out, assisting Alicia as she grabs one arm and helps her waddle across the porch on her crutches.

"These are for you." Cyn gives Lorene a bouquet of roses.

Lorene inhales the odor and instructs Graham to put the flowers in a vase with water. About that time, Sam arrives on a motorcycle.

When everyone is inside the house, and coats and scarfs hung in the hall closet, Lorene makes sure Alicia is seated comfortably in the den while she attends the duties required to complete Thanksgiving dinner. Graham has brought a bottle of red wine and prepares glasses for a toast. Papa Perkins is not present, but not forgotten.

"Here's a toast to my daddy!" Graham raises his goblet. "To the best man I ever knew! A great husband and father!"

"I'll drink to that!" Lorene gulps down the wine. It burns all the way down her throat, but she doesn't care. Mark Hagen is also in his grave; Dorothy made sure of that. And Clint Howard helped.

* * *

Ellie went home for Thanksgiving. Lloyd opted not to face her mother and a hundred questions about the honeymoon he had planned. He was taking two weeks off following the wedding and they were flying to London, England, with a short excursion to France.

There was no way he'd tell Ellie's parents about the trip. Jasmine could not keep a secret. And she'd ruin the surprise for Ellie.

It's already dark outside when he locks up his office and exits the building. Not much open on Thanksgiving after noon, so he drives through town looking for a fast-food restaurant. Many are closed.

It's lonely without Ellie. He walks up a flight of stairs to his apartment. He's spoken to Dorothy Perkins about selling her property, but she believes it's not the right time to move when the house has just been redecorated at the expense of All State Insurance Company.

He opens the door and steps inside. The light switch is on the wall to his right. As he reaches to turn on the lights, he feels the cold butt of a pistol in his side. "Good evening, Detective."

Lloyd raises his hands. "Can I help you with something?"

"You sure can."

Lloyd hears the explosion, but what is happening does not register until he feels a hole in his side oozing with liquid. *Blood.*

Dizziness. Staggering forward. Then nothing.

Dom tosses a flaming match and locks the door behind him.

33

CLAIRE'S FAMILY HAVE ALL gone home by ten p.m. It was a fantastic day and the Thanksgiving meal was superb. I've decided to spend the night rather than drive home in the dark. Clouds have gathered in the sky and a cold front has created foggy conditions. My cell phone rings just as I crawl under the bedsheets in hopes of a good night's sleep.

"Dorothy, are you sitting down?"

"No, Lorene, I'm lying down. What's the problem?"

"I, uh . . ." there is emotion trapped in her few words.

"Just tell me, Lorene." I fear word has come that Tom is dead. But how would she know? The CIA wouldn't call her.

"It's about Detective Peters."

"What about him?" I yawn, ready to call it a day.

"He's dead."

I sit up in bed and kick off the covers. "What happened?"

"Sam called me. He thought I should know."

"Because you would tell me." I understood his reasoning.

"No details about what happened?" A heart attack came to mind. Butch was always uptight. "Was he involved in a car accident?"

"No, Dorothy, he was shot!"

"With a gun?"

"How else can you be shot?" Lorene returns.

"I'm coming home." I get up and start dressing.

"There's more."

"What could be worse than getting shot, Lorene?"

"Someone set fire to his apartment with him inside."

"Before or after he was shot?" I wanted more information.

"I don't know. Sam was working the nightshift at the Fire Department. He called me right after the EMTs took his body away.

"What about Ellie?" I inquire.

"No one has mentioned her," Lorene replies.

"I'm coming home. We'll sort out this mess." I wonder if I'm in danger, too. Is this payback by the Russian Mafia? My imagination runs wild for several seconds, and I discover I am visibly trembling.

"I don't recommend driving in this fog," Lorene says to me.

I realize Claire is standing in the doorway.

"It's Lorene," I tell her.

My daughter is not leaving without an explanation.

I listen to a few more details Sam passed on to Lorene then end the call. "I have to go home, Claire. Butch Peters was shot and killed. His apartment was set afire—I suppose to destroy forensic evidence."

"What?" Claire splays her hands. "No, Mama! Stay out of it!"

"Yes, Claire. I'm certain the Russian Mafia are involved." I check my purse to see that I have everything as I slip into my loafers without socks. I don't have time to dress properly. It's not like I'll see Tom.

"I'll go with you," Claire says.

"No, I'm going to Lorene's first then we'll decide on what to do next." My thoughts are scattered and the unknown is frightening.

* * *

TBI Special Agent in Charge Stanley Kilpatrick is notified of the shooting at Detective Lloyd Peter's apartment. Currently, he stands on the street as the apartment fire spreads to the entire second floor.

He spies a vehicle with Sheriff's Office attached to the side door. Captain Marilyn Colbert opens the passenger door and steps out.

Stan waves at her. *Over here . . .* he motions.

Her expression says she's less than pleased over the incident.

"I know . . ." they bump fists, a salutation contrived since Covid-19 assaulted the world and turned every day into a pandemic.

"Happy Thanksgiving," she mutters. "What've we got here?"

"Arson and murder," Stan replies.

"Why were you called first?" Marilyn glares at the agent.

"It's believed the hit is associated with the Russian Mafia," he explains as jet sprays from large hoses blanket the rooftop of the burning complex. "Detective Peters was read in on our sting."

"I know." Marilyn heaves a sigh. "Hate to see it end for him like this." She thinks of Ellie Simpson. "Has his secretary been notified?"

"No one seems to know where she is," he replies.

"Do you think harm has come to her, too?"

"No reason to believe that, Captain Colbert." He scratches his neck as the fog turns into a light rain. "I'll give you a call tomorrow."

"Okay," she says, "I see no reason to hang around tonight."

"Has the Medical Examiner been contacted?" Stan asks. "She will need to process the body first thing in the morning. A fireman told me Peters had a hole in his stomach, but did not know if he was shot before or after the fire was set. Good way to eliminate forensic evidence." DNA was linked to individuals through data systems.

"Can't believe this is happening to our quaint community."

Stan shakes his head. "Well, I'm tired, so I'm heading home."

"Back to Nashville?" Marilyn notes the thickening fog.

"Yes, I've driven in worse weather."

* * *

I tap on Lorene's front door a tad before midnight. The foggy air is thick with humidity and it's freezing. Lorene opens the door, sleepy-eyed and distraught. "Sorry to cut your visit with Claire short."

"I'm glad you phoned me with the news."

We go into the den together, Lorene shuffling across the wood floors in her fluffy-pink slippers that match her housecoat.

The television is broadcasting on mute.

"This is terrible!" I sigh as I collapse in her recliner.

"What do you think it means?" Lorene perches on the arm of the sofa, her right foot dobbing up and down with her every heartbeat.

"For us, or for me?"

"Both? If it's the Russian Mafia, are they going to kill us, too?"

"Not if I can help it." I'm angry and ready to face off with the enemy, wishing Tom could give me his best strategy to confront evil.

"Should we call Ellie?" Lorene asks.

"Surely, the police have already done that."

"Is there any way we can find out for sure?" Lorene asks.

"Tom works for the CIA. Do you still have that number?"

"Yes, I wrote it down before I gave the card to Claire." Lorene locates her booklet with names of friends, their addresses, and phone numbers. We're too old to trust phones with our information.

"Here it is." Lorene reads off the number as I punch in the digits. I wait and finally a voice answers: "CIA, how may I direct you?"

"Thomas Kessler," I reply.

I am promptly put on hold.

"Director Jackson Carlton, who's calling?"

"Dorothy Powell. I want to speak to Thomas Kessler."

Silence is so somber I think he's hung up on me.

"Director Carlton, there's been an incident," I say.

No response. I need to explain further.

"Detective Lloyd Peters was murdered tonight in his apartment in Colombia, Tennessee, shot and killed, his apartment set on fire."

He knows a lot of profanity. I wait for his tirade to end.

"Is there any way I can find out if Detective Peter's secretary, Ellie Simpson, has been notified? They're engaged."

"I'll make some calls and get back to you."

A few seconds pass.

"Are you related to Ellie, Ms. Powell?"

"No, but she's a good friend. Someone who cares about her should tell her what's happened." I run out of words.

He abruptly ends the call. I frown.

But Lorene is grinning. "I don't think you made his day."

"Too bad." All I care about is Ellie.

Lorene yawns. "Sleep with me in my bed tonight."

"Gladly." I have no desire to go up the stairs alone. Two against one have better odds. *Oh, Arthur! I wish you were here to protect us.*

34

Friday, November 25

ON THANKSGIVING DAY, TWO years ago, I had scattered Arthur's ashes on our farm's pasture. No one had sat in his chair at our dining room table since that day. Today will set a new precedent.

Claire, her husband Ted, their two children, and my grandchildren are due at my house for the celebration meal. The Pilgrims started the tradition when they settled in America, the land of the free.

Yet, why didn't I feel free?

Evil, immoral people, male and female, roam the streets of America in dark corners seeking to steal the peace and property of ordinary citizens. Professionals working for organizations like the TBI, the FBI, and CIA are hired to protect the innocent, but fail when perpetrators receive big payment for their acts of violence.

"Dorothy?"

I spin around in the barstool and see Lorene standing there, still dressed in night trappings. "It's four a.m., why are you up?"

I stare into the dregs clinging to the bottom of my mug, the remnant of last night's reheated coffee. "Just thinking."

Her lips part slightly, but she says nothing.

I stiffen. "And don't you dare say, *Penny for your thoughts!* Mine are far too heavy to share this morning."

She slumps over to the barstool and mounts it. "I wasn't."

"You don't have to get up this early just because I did."

"I know, but we should make plans for the day," she says.

"First of all, how about a real cup of fresh Folger's to jumpstart your morning?" I feel like rewarding my best friend and neighbor.

"Sure."

I love Lorene. What would I do without her?

I make the coffee and we carry our mugs steeped in real cream and sugar into the den and sit down. Lorene switches on a news channel. We wait for a reporter to update the public on the shooting of a prominent Columbia resident, Detective Lloyd Peters.

I hear a cock crow and am surprised.

"You have a rooster?" Lorene's barn was blown down.

"Sam put up a makeshift shed and gave me Blackhawk and four hens." Lorene giggles. "The feisty rooster rules the roost."

"Just what you need, another animal to look after." I am suddenly reminded of my pet. "Who's keeping Pepper if Ellie is not home?"

She'd offered to watch the little pup over Thanksgiving.

"We can't ask Butch. And we don't know where Ellie is."

"Well, that should be number one on today's TO-DO list," I proclaim. "I'll use the bathroom upstairs to shower and get dressed."

* * *

Ellie Simpson unlocks the door to her apartment and flips on the lights. Everything looks just as she'd left it, in a huge mess since she'd left Dorothy's dog off at the vet on Wednesday and decided to catch a flight to Chicago and spend a few quality days with her parents.

They lived twenty miles east of the city, so she'd rented a car and driven to their mansion in the countryside. Lloyd hadn't come with her because he'd insisted on completing his file on Lorita Willems.

But the fact he wasn't answering his cell this morning before she left Chicago worried her. Did he binge drink last night? Out at the bars enjoying bachelorhood as long as he could? He wouldn't sleep with another woman. She'd kill him if she found out and he knew that.

No, something else was going on. *What?*

It was six a.m. Too early to go into the office, so Ellie unpacks her bag and puts on a load of clothes to wash. She's in no mood to hear the bad news reported every morning, so the TV stays off.

The plane flight was uneventful, the airways smooth. All is quiet in sleepy Columbia, Tennessee. *Not a bad thing*, she thinks.

After taking a bubble bath and dressing, she removes her cell phone from her purse. The battery has crashed. It will take at least fifteen minutes to charge. She sits in the den, dwelling on the day.

Turning on the cell, Ellie notes multiple messages: voice mails and texts showing up. She returns one call, a bit worried.

"This is Ellie Simpson, Captain Colbert. You left me a voice message saying it was urgent to return your call," she says.

"Ms. Simpson, is it too early for me to come over?"

"To my apartment?" Ellie is surprised. "Has something happened that involves me?" Her mind races to Lloyd, is he hurt?

140

"Yes, I'll come over, or we could meet at your office."

"I was going there early, anyhow. I'll leave now."

Ellie collects her belongings, dons a coat since it's frosty outdoors, locks her apartment, and drives to the precinct. She's worked as Lloyd's secretary for five years and counting. She's loved him four-and-a-half years of that time. His conviction to maintain order in society is strong. Underneath all that vibrato lies a kind-hearted man.

Ellie believes they are a good match. He's distrusted relationships most of his life. His father beat him and his mother did nothing to stop the abuse. It is a miracle he turned out so well. His first marriage failed, but so had hers. Sometimes it takes a few tries to get a relationship right. What's important is not giving up. There is a right partner for everyone. God ordains that man should not live alone.

The drive to the office seems longer than usual. Ellie spies Captain Marilyn Colbert's squad car parked out front in the guest space.

They exit their vehicles at the same time. It's quarter to eight, but Officer Joe has already unlocked the front door and lets them inside.

"Pretty cold out there this morning," he comments, tipping his hat to the doctor with a degree in Criminal Law. She's black with a stocky figure and a no-nonsense personality. Columbia is darn lucky to have her overseeing its residents. "Detective Peters hasn't come in."

"Thank you, Officer Kelly." Marilyn leads the way to the elevator.

Ellie steps aboard, troubled by the urgent early meeting, and the fact that Lloyd has not been invited to attend. The elevator shudders as it halts on the second floor and the double doors slide open.

They exit and walk down the hall.

"Captain Colbert, am I in trouble?" Ellie asks.

"No, of course not!" She points to the door.

"Oh." Ellie unlocks the office and they step inside.

"Turn on some lights and make us coffee, Ms. Simpson."

"Ellie, please." She knows her way around the kitchen and fills the Keurig machine with tap water, then switches it on.

"Sure, and for this meeting, I'm simply Marilyn."

The water heats as the machine groans slightly. Ellie realizes that this meeting with Captain Colbert is quite serious. Nobody calls the Captain of the Columbia Police Department by her first name.

Nobody.

"Make mine strong and black," Marilyn orders.

Ellie's hand is shaking as she places the Keurig cup in its holder and closes the top. The machine will do the rest. The hot water spews through the coffee grounds and creates a pleasant odor in the kitchen.

When both have mugs of comfort in their hands, they go into Lloyd's office. Marilyn sits at his desk; Ellie pulls up a chair.

"I'm sorry to inform you that Detective Lloyd Peters was shot and killed in his apartment last night," Marilyn informs Ellie. "A fire was set so he's almost unrecognizable. I'm so sorry for your loss."

Ellie sits there calmly, thinking she has not heard right. Was she still in bed, asleep and in the middle of the worst nightmare of her life?

"I'm sorry, what did you just say?" Shock is setting in.

"Lloyd is dead."

Ellie blinks. She feels dizzy. "I—"

The next thing she knows she's waking up on the floor of Lloyd's office. A medic is standing over. Tears tumble like heavy raindrops as she sits up and tries to cope with the news. "Where is he?"

"At the morgue. He'll be processed and cremated"

Ellie's world has just crashed. All she can see in front of her is a black hole, a void she wants to crawl into and disappear. It would be better if she had not been born than to experience this kind of loss.

* * *

"Ellie's still not answering her cell phone," I tell Lorene. They are at Cracker Barrel finishing up a country-ham breakfast. I don't care if I gain twenty pounds. I need my comfort food today. Arthur is dead. Tom is gone. Butch, now murdered. What else bad will happen?

"How are we going to find Pepper?" Lorene asks.

"Well, if Ellie doesn't have him, she probably took him to Yancy's Veterinarian Services." YVS for short on his marquee.

"Okay, we'll drive over there and check."

"I'll get our meal, Lorene. You've done enough for me."

"No problem, what are friends for?"

"Speaking of friends . . ." Dorothy hands the server her credit card. "How is Alicia coping with her broken leg?"

"She has a full-time nanny staying part days and every night."

"Anyone I know?"

"Zoey Jackson."

"My Lord! I have not even called that child." I wonder if another college tuition payment is due. All my energy has been centered on Clint Howard, a.k.a. Thomas Kessler. I sign the payment slip and add a healthy tip. These young, ambitious servers need to know they are appreciated. "First things first. Let's go find my pup," I say.

We are in Lorene's green Tesla and she's driving.

Fifteen minutes later we are parked at YVS.

"Sit in the car. I'll go inside and ask about Pepper," I volunteer.

Lorene waits in the car with the heat running while music is playing on the radio. Ten minutes goes by before she sees a smiling Dorothy walk out the front door of Yancy's holding a wiggling, yelping Yorkshire Terrier snuggly in her arms. The car door opens.

"I found him and paid his tab!" I fill the passenger seat.

"Great! What's our next task?"

"Let's drive over to my house. I want to see how the repairs are progressing. I can pick up Pepper's food supplies in the shed and then we'll go back to your house, if two guests aren't too much for you."

"Of course not, Pepper's part of the family."

"Hooray! We have a pup and a rooster!" I exclaim with glee.

35

DESPITE CAPTAIN COLBERT'S WARNING that Lloyd Peters' body is unrecognizable, Ellie Simpson insists on seeing him at the morgue.

They are riding together in the squad car. Marilyn is driving. Ellie is too shaky and upset to be behind the wheel of a moving vehicle.

"He may have already been cremated," Marilyn cautions Ellie. "Let me take you home. You need to grieve privately."

Ellie knows Marilyn is right but still she needs to see that Lloyd is really dead, or her heart will never accept the loss.

Marilyn parks in front of the building that houses the morgue in its basement. Ambulances arrive at a side door to bring in gurneys carrying the deceased. M.E. Cynthia Preston and her staff process the bodies, either send them to the funeral home where they are prepped for burial, or a family member picks up the urn with the human ashes.

Ellie dreads seeing Lloyd, but she must. She has to . . .

"Two more murders came in today," Dr. Preston comments to Captain Colbert as Ellie walks with them down a long hallway. The offensive formaldehyde odor and remnants of dead flesh make Ellie want to vomit. She tries to keep it together and get the job done.

"He's in here." The M.E. points through an open doorway.

Ellie doesn't wait to be invited inside. She goes straight over to the slab of concrete and pulls back the sheet. Lloyd's face is caved in, black with soot. His cheeks have melted into his skull.

It's him. Or was. Ellie covers his body and staggers, feeling faint.

"It's him," she utters, bent over, tears dripping on the floor.

Cynthia, younger than Marilyn, assists Ellie back to the squad car. "We are so sorry for your loss. I understand you were to be married."

"Yes, Christmas Eve." Ellie still needs to call her parents.

* * *

Lorene parks her Tesla in front of Dorothy's farmhouse. There is no activity going on at this time. "Where are the carpenters?"

"Well, at least the roof is back," I note. "Let's see if the backdoor is open. Pull around to the shed so I can get Pepper's stuff."

"Yes, ma'am."

"Maybe, I should let him out to pee," I decide.

Lorene backs up in the gravel and moves forward again.

"I'll also get a larger cage for Pepper," I say. "Punch the button to lift the trunk." I set the little toot on the ground to run around the backyard. He's happy as a lark in spring as he hikes to pee on a stump.

After I load a bag of Puppy Chow in the trunk of Lorene's car with his larger cage, I slam the door and pick up Pepper. Lorene is already on the back porch trying to open the door to the kitchen.

"Get the key under the flower pot!" I call out loudly.

She bends over and shows me a shiny key. "Your security system is not going to protect you from prowlers if you hide a key out here."

"I know, it's for the carpenters." I approach the porch holding tightly to Pepper. Lorene opens the door. We both smell fresh wood and paint. My den is intact and the walls are painted the light color of gray as I requested. The Old Pine wood floors are brand new.

"That's a fancy light fixture!" Lorene points overhead.

My new round kitchen table with six chairs will sit under it.

"The contractor texted me my choices," I explain to Lorene.

She smiles. "You were too busy dating Clint Howard to oversee your own decorations personally. Are you in love again, Dorothy?"

How can I lie to my best friend?

"I am in love with the idea of love," I answer. "I never told you that I look like Clint's first wife Angela." It's time for clarity.

"No wonder you blew him away," she says.

I place Pepper on the floor to run around and investigate every interesting odor. "I need to put the past month behind me."

"We all do," Lorene agrees. "Do you think he loves you?"

"If I were Angela, yes. But I'm not. I'm a version of her, but much older. He wanted to believe I can be her, but I can't."

Lorene nodded. "That's truly sad."

"I know."

"You were just getting over Arthur's death and now you're grieving all over again," she says. "I'm so sorry for your loss."

"Thank you, my friend." Life has many facets of emotions. Joy, sadness, boldness, fear—the human spirit experiences a wide range of feelings. Will that come to an end at death? Or continue into the Afterlife? Those are questions only time and patience will answer.

We lock up the house and drive over to visit Alicia Colby. Zoey answers the door. "Oh, sweetheart! I'm so pleased to see you." I give her a hug. "I was going to call you, but life has me in the fast track."

"I heard about Detective Peters," the young woman says. "My boyfriend is a Volunteer Fireman and works with Sam Perkins."

"My son?" Lorene chimes in. "How's our patient?"

"I'm right here!" Alicia calls out from the sofa. "Do I hear a pup yelping." She looks at me. "Is that Pepper? Bring him to me."

"I'll get him out of the car," Lorene volunteers.

"Zoey, make us some hot tea, we have guests," Alicia says.

"Yes, ma'am."

We sit in the compact living room, a fire leaping in the hearth to warm the room. I am comforted to have friends surrounding me, a cup of herbal tea with honey and lemon in my hands, and hope that tomorrow will bring better thoughts and more love to our community.

36

Saturday, November 26

I KNOCKED ON ELLIE'S apartment door for the longest time. About to decide she is not home the door suddenly opens.

"You!" Ellie looks less than pleased.

For a few seconds, I ponder her surly attitude. "I'm so sorry for your loss." I hand her the pie Lorene made earlier today. "Butch wasn't my favorite person, but he did not deserve to be murdered." I am far too honest for the grieving woman.

Her hand draws back and before I know it, my left cheek is stinging. Ellie is right-handed. She has slapped me.

I rub away the pain and take the abuse with courage.

"It's your fault Lloyd is dead!" Ellie screams at me.

I consider if I'm still in bed at Lorene's house and this is a nightmare. When Ellie slaps me silly again, I decide this is the real deal.

I shove Ellie back inside the apartment with one hand while the pie dangles in the other. I'm several inches taller and weigh a good thirty pounds more than she does, so it really is no contest.

I have the presence to place the pie on the coffee table before I drop it. "Blame me if you wish, Ellie. I did not come here to fight you."

She stumbles backward a few steps, tears streaking her cheeks.

"I don't know what else to say, Ellie."

We let the awkward moment linger. It's her turn.

"Lloyd considered it his job to protect you, Dorothy. Did you know that?" She scrubs her cheeks with both hands. "He never should have gone to that safehouse in Crossville. I'm so furious at him."

"So, you're taking your fury out on me?" I glance around the apartment. Ellie has been packing. "You're moving?"

"Yes, back to Chicago to be near my parents."

She goes into the kitchen and begins making coffee. Hoping she won't pull a gun on me, I follow her. "Can I help in any way?"

Ellie blinks. "I'm lost without him, Dorothy!"

I want to hold the grieving woman in my arms and attempt to provide comfort, but she wouldn't let me. "I felt the same way when Arthur was murdered two years ago. But, honey, life must go on."

"Not mine!" She stiffens as the Keurig Coffeemaker heats up.

"When did you eat last?" I ask. The woman is skinny as a rail. I investigate her pantry. "You don't have much food in store."

"I've been letting my stock go down, planning on moving with Lloyd after we marry." She angrily glares at me. "Your house."

"Ellie, I told Butch I wasn't ready to sell."

"Lloyd! Don't call him Butch. He hated it."

I could not win today any way I tried.

"Why don't you pack a bag and come home with me," I suggest. "You don't need to be alone at a time like this."

"You don't have a home." Ellie hands me my cup of coffee. "Cream is in the fridge; sugar in that bowl." She brews hers.

"Lorene Perkins does, and you are most welcome."

Ellie sadly looks around. "I have so much packing to do. Then I've got to clean up before my parents arrive. We are having a memorial service for Lloyd next Wednesday. But thanks for the invite."

"Look . . ." I was never one to give up, "come with me for just one night and let's talk about what happened to Lloyd. I don't know how much he told you, but I can fill in some details." I pause.

She says nothing, deep in speculation.

"On Monday, Lorene and I will come over here with you and help pack and clean up," I promise. "Be sensible. Please, Ellie."

She pitifully glares at me. "Lloyd always saw promise in you, Dorothy. I think he secretly wanted to please you."

I melted like hot Swiss cheese. "That is so sweet of you to say that, Ellie. Even though you hate me for my part in this fiasco."

"It's not really your fault Lloyd was murdered."

"I know, but I do feel responsible—why else am I here?"

Ellie suddenly lunges at me, holds me so tight I can hardly breathe.

"Oh, Dorothy, I am so devastated I don't know what to do." The tears come in torrents and I can do nothing to stop them.

I let her weep on my shoulder and blame the universe for its unkindness until she is weak and totally spent. "I'm done."

"I know. Now, let's pack you a bag and come with me."

* * *

Ellie slept all morning in Lorene's guest bedroom upstairs. Poor thing was exhausted from the last few days of grieving for her fiancé, a man she would never marry or give him children. I am downstairs in the kitchen with Lorene as she makes chicken sandwiches for lunch.

"I don't know how you think you can help Ellie," Lorene tells me. "She is angry at you for roping Detective Peters into your fiasco."

I watch as she adds cheese and mayo on two sandwiches.

"Wait a minute, partner!" I take exception. "Butch asked us to spy on Alicia Colby, or have you forgotten? He started this mess."

"No, no . . ." she shakes a knife at me, "the CIA started this mess when they turned a killer loose on you. Or did you forget?"

"I hope you're not blaming Tom for my troubles."

"Who's Tom?"

Lorene and I turn around and spy a sleepy green-eyed Ellie standing in the archway between the den and kitchen.

"Come in, sweetheart. You can have my sandwich," I say.

She throws a hand, "No, thanks, not hungry. Who's Tom?"

"Thomas Kessler," Lorene answers for me.

"His alias is Clint Howard," I qualify. "He was an undercover spy for the CIA, sent to Columbia to protect me from Mark Hagen."

Ellie scoffs, "Fine job he did! You were abducted and now Lloyd is dead. I understand he took a bullet for you."

All of this information is extremely painful. I feel guilt, and none of what has happened is my fault. I don't know what to say.

"Look," Lorene intervenes, "we all need to try and make some sense out of what's happened in our small sleepy town."

"I know what's happened!" Ellie barks. "Evil came to visit."

And I hope not stay, I think to myself. *Am I still in danger?*

"Where's Pepper?" Ellie takes a seat at the bar.

"In his crate on the back porch. It's sunny today and I thought the fresh air would do him good," I answer. "Thanks for watching after him while I couldn't." Lorene makes a sandwich for Ellie.

"Ice tea or soda?" she inquires.

"Sweet tea, please." Ellie accepts the plate and bows her head to pray over her food. "I'm sorry I'm in such a foul mood."

"You're entitled," I say. "You should know I figured out who murdered Lorita Willems." Ellie nearly drops her sandwich.

"You told Lloyd?"

"Yes," I reply. "While I was abducted and kept at the Mafia's safehouse in Crossville, Mark Hagen commented to his boss, 'Watch out, she may give you poison tea.' Why would he say that unless he was the one who sent the tea to Lorita? It had to be him."

Ellie nods. "That makes sense, then he comes after you."

"Lorita was always a powder keg to the Mafia. She was close to her half-brother Clyde, so it made sense he told her everything."

"Including the names of the Mafia bosses he hid?" Ellie says, and takes a bite of her sandwich. The bride that was is ravenously hungry.

"We're worried about you," I tell the young woman.

Ellie licks mayo off her fingers. "I've been slapped down before."

"We want you to rest here a couple of days, then on Monday, like I promised, we will help you clean your apartment and pack."

"I should get out of Dodge? The ruffians are coming?"

"Something like that." I wonder if Ellie's comment is an omen that I should personally take seriously. My cell phone rings.

"Hello."

I listen then say, "The repairs have been completed on my house," I tell the girls. "I can move back in."

"Oh, I don't know, Dorothy. You, alone, in the house?"

"You're right, I should talk to Claire first."

37

Sunday, November 27

CLAIRE AND TED CAME over early Sunday afternoon and went through a checklist of repairs with me. My deductible was generous, but I had opted to upgrade for a renovated kitchen with tile flooring and granite countertops. Claire thought if I ever decided to sell, the improvements would help bring top dollar. We were about to have more company. Wes and Jasmine Parks were on their way.

Alicia Colby and Ellie Simpson sit together on the sofa. The television—a huge wide-screen that upstages the room—is turned off.

Ted thought I should have the biggest and best, so he paid the difference as a gift. The Old Pine floors were of my choosing.

Lorene sits at my new bar. The opening between the breakfast room and kitchen leaves the space wide open. No wallpaper again. But I selected a light blue for the entire house. I hate beige, so boring.

I hear a knock at my front door. "I'll get it," Claire offers.

A pot of herbal spiced tea sits on the eye of my new gas range. The oven is also gas, a financial savings Claire says, and I trust her judgment. I love my daughter. I love that Ted calls me Mama now.

Ellie seems to wake up from her dreamworld as she sees her mother and father walk into the den. "Oh, Mama . . ." she gushes tears. They embrace like they have been away from one another a long time. I know it has only been a few days. Ellie came home on Thursday.

"I'm Dorothy Powell," I introduce myself to Wes and Jasmine.

"It's so nice of you to open your home to us," Jasmine says. "Ellie tells me you have been taking good care of her."

"Wes." He shakes my hand. Ellie's father is gangly and reminds me of strawman in the Wizard of Oz. His hair is thick and unruly, white as Santa Claus's, and his bushy eyebrows are a perfect match.

In contrast, Jasmine is petite like Ellie. She can't weigh over one-hundred and twenty pounds. Eyes a deep blue-gray, her bobbed hair has been colored a light shade of blond. It's easy to see where Ellie gets her beauty genes from, though her father gushes with character.

"Welcome to Columbia. Sorry it's under such sad circumstances," I tell Wes, my gaze shifting to Jasmine. "Will you join us for tea?"

"I thought I smelled cinnamon," Wes says as he hugs his daughter.

"Mother, I'm so sorry about the wedding," Ellie says.

"No, dear, that's not a problem. We cancelled everything. Nobody blames us, or you, for unforeseeable circumstances," Jasmine says.

Ellie nods, tears poised to flow again.

Ted has set a fire in the hearth and my house smells so new I wish Arthur were here to enjoy the renovations. Life is in motion.

"I'll get the beverages." Lorene abandons her perch on a barstool. While she fills six mugs, I open a plastic container of oatmeal cookies and place them on the bar with a stack of colorful napkins.

Wes wants to hear all about Lloyd's death, but Ellie has no information. "It's an ongoing investigation, Daddy," she explains.

"Did the Mafia do this?" Jasmine inquires while sipping tea.

Alicia has said nothing to this point. "We'll get the buzzards."

Her response is so out of British character Lorene and I laugh.

"Well, we will!" Alicia gushes.

"I hope so," Ellie peeps from the new recliner with an electric gizmo to tilt it back. Arthur's old one is gone, out with the storm.

So much has changed in a month. October, two years ago, was a nightmare. This October was equally challenging. I met a man I could love, only to discover he was still in love with his first wife. A deceased woman who looked like me thirty years ago. And now Tom's gone and probably never coming back. I empathize with Ellie's profound grief.

"Ted and I brought supper for all of us," Claire says. "I hope you like Kentucky Fried Chicken with all the trimmings."

"What kind of trimmings?" Alicia curiously asks.

"Cream potatoes, green beans, coleslaw," Ted replies.

"It sounds marvelous to me," I comment.

We talk for another forty-five minutes as the gray day grows dark and thick fog sets in. "Let's dine," Lorene says. "I need to go home."

"Me, too," Alicia says, shivering as if a cold wind blew through.

"No," Lorene looks at her, "you're staying the night with me."

I laugh. "You girls scared I won't be there to protect you?"

"Everyone had better be scared," Ellie stoically remarks.

"No, honey, you're safe with us," Wes tells his daughter. "Your mother and I will never let any bad man touch you. We promise."

Ellie is fortunate to have such loving parents.

And I love that my friends are so caring. I am alone now that Arthur is not with me. But I have family I can count on.

We have supper then Lorene helps Alicia to her Tesla.

"Call me when you get home," I tell them.

"We will," Alicia says from the passenger seat.

I close the car door for her. "Talk to you tomorrow," I tell Lorene as she switches on the motor. "Drive safely in this fog."

"We will," Alicia replies.

I stand on my porch steps and watch the car disappear into the approaching darkness. I find the kitchen tidy when I return. We'd used paper products so cleanup was easy.

"Anyone for decaf coffee?" I offer.

"I'd love some," Jasmine replies.

We pig out on a chocolate cake from the Sweet Delights, a dessert shop that recently opened up on Columbia's town square.

Bedtime is at nine tonight. Wes and Jasmine accompany Ellie upstairs to my guest bedrooms. As I retire to my bedroom, I miss Arthur even more. Tom brightened my life like a firecracker going off.

I giggle as I crawl under the covers.

"Sweet dreams," I tell myself as I switch off the bedside lamp.

38

Wednesday, November 30

I AM UP EARLY TO prepare breakfast for my guests. On Monday, Lorene and I, with the help of Wes and Jasmine, packed Ellie's apartment for pickup by the moving company on Thursday. Alicia went home with Lorene yesterday but said she couldn't hide from the bad guys forever and would be back in her log cabin by lunch today.

When everyone leaves and resumes their normal lives, I wonder if I'll be able to cope with loneliness again. I open a can of Folgers.

"Good morning, Dorothy."

After filling the coffeemaker with ten cups of water, and measuring out the coffee grounds to the cupholder, I turn on the coffeemaker and see Jasmine standing there in her PJ's and housecoat.

"Coffee will be ready shortly," I tell her, trying to smile.

"I can't tell you how much Wes and I appreciate your hospitality, Dorothy." She sits at my new bar in a padded barstool, an upgrade.

"No problem." I sigh. "I welcome the company."

"You'll owe us a visit soon."

"Thank you. How did our girl sleep last night?"

"Not well. I heard her weeping throughout the night," Jasmine reports. "Wes went into her bedroom twice to comfort her."

I blink with tears. "There's little comfort for losing someone you love dearly," I empathize. "But Ellie has you, and she's a survivor."

"I know you only know my daughter professionally, but she's had a difficult life," Jasmine begins to share private family information.

I listen as the story of Ellie unfolds. She had a teenage pregnancy and gave up a little boy for adoption. Then married her boyfriend, who turned out to be a real jerk and distributed illegal drugs to teens. She only stayed with him a few years before divorce was inevitable. Her second marriage went no better—the guy cheated on her.

"She was just finding happiness with Lloyd," Jasmine continues. "He was rough on the edges but I know he loved my daughter."

"I know he did, too," I say as the coffee bubbles out in the glass container. "Cream and sugar this morning?"

"I try to watch my figure, but yes, today I want the works."

We respectively fix our coffees and go out on the front porch to view the new day. The sun is just turning the dewy morning sky to a rusty color as clouds begin to dissipate as if fleeing from the brightness.

I think of Thomas Kessler and wonder where he is, if he's looking up at the sky from a foreign country where he plots a clandestine mission. He's clever, I give him that. I sigh and Jasmine notices.

"You seem heavy-hearted today," she tells me.

"I am. I've lost someone I care a lot about."

"Ellie's told me some of what you've been through with the CIA and that murderous Mark Hagen. At least, he's dead."

"May I ask your opinion on something?"

"Sure." Jasmine folds her body and sits on the porch steps.

"Given a guess, who do you think murdered Lloyd?" I do not say *Butch*, out of respect to the dead. "Does he have enemies other than the Russian Mafia?" I despise I'm even considering solving this crime.

"A detective always has enemies," she replies. "He's arrested numerous criminals over his career of thirty years with the Columbia Police Department." We hear the door open behind us.

I face a bleary-eyed young woman. "Ellie."

"Mama? Do you think someone local murdered Lloyd?"

Jasmine sets her mug on the steps and slowly rises. "I don't know, dear. But we should not assume the Mafia killed him."

"You're right."

"I don't want you to worry about that," Jasmine says.

"I can't help it. Daddy says he's hungry."

"I am, too. Let's go inside and I'll whip up an omelet and place some biscuits in the oven to bake. I have fresh blackberry jam and apple butter my card buddy Lizzy brought over yesterday."

"Sounds delicious," Jasmine said as we went back inside.

* * *

The memorial service for Lloyd was scheduled for two p.m. at the Civic Center. I have never seen so many men and women in police uniforms as they file down the aisle and find seats. There are also dignitaries from Nashville and representatives from the FBI. I wondered if any of them are CIA incognito. *Is Tom here?*

It's a long service, multiple people speaking on behalf of Lloyd as the man and the professional detective. I try to concentrate and find it difficult. I keep thinking about Tom and wonder if he survived the gunshot intended for me. I pray he did. Will he ever come back to Columbia to see me? I doubt he will. As far as he's concerned the CIA has accomplished their mission through him.

I realize everyone is standing and applauding. I feel Claire's hand on my elbow. "Mama, are you okay?"

"Yes, dear." I give her a light hug. "Thanks for coming."

"I didn't want you to go home alone following the service."

I nod. Wes and Jasmine were driving Ellie to Nashville and staying at a fancy hotel until it was time to meet the movers on Friday. It was a good idea. Out with the old, in with the new.

As we get into Claire's Buick, I notice a man standing on the sidewalk across the street. He seems to be staring at us.

Claire starts the motor and pulls into the traffic.

"Did you see that man watching us?" I ask, turning around in my seat to see if he was still standing there. He wasn't.

"Now, Mama, don't get paranoid on me. You have a first-class security system at your beautiful newly-renovated house."

"I swear he was watching us."

"Okay. We're going back to your house, and you're packing a bag and coming home with me for the weekend," Claire insists. "I'm watching my grandchildren, and I can certainly use some help."

"Okay, fine." I won't argue, especially after seeing a suspicious character watching me. What could he possibly want? I have no lists or knowledge of anything clandestine to share with anyone.

39

Four days before Christmas

IT'S MY TURN TO treat my family to Christmas dinner. Besides my family, I have invited Lorene and Alicia to join us. Sam Perkins has to work at the fire station and begged off. Graham Perkins and his wife, Dr. Cynthia Preston, our illustrious coroner, accepted my invitation.

It's a cold, brisk day but no snow forecast, thank God. I ordered a huge turkey with dressing from Kroger's Deli that was delivered an hour ago and is warming in the oven. Claire made sweet potato casserole and fresh cranberry relish. My granddaughter Helen brought a green-bean casserole and homemade yeast rolls.

Alicia insisted on bringing something, so I told her to bring some English tea we can enjoy following our meal. Lorene contributed two jugs of tea, one with sugar the other with Splenda. My son-in-law Ted pretends to be on a diet, but I'd bet my last dollar he has two desserts.

Benjamin's girlfriend made two pies, one pecan and the other apple. We are all set to pig out and open presents.

It's eleven a.m. and everyone is arriving on schedule. Ted takes their coats and hangs them either on the foyer tree or in the coat closet under the staircase. I am the hostess with the most-est.

Because it gets dark so early in December, I thought it better to have our celebration at noon. I decided not to hold a chair for Arthur this year. He's quite comfortable in his Heavenly home, probably seated in a recliner looking down on all of us with a smile on his face.

"Mama, you have a phone call." She hands me my cell.

"Hello?"

"It's Ellie Simpson calling from New York," I tell her then walk down the hall to the foyer so I can hear better.

"Merry Christmas, Dorothy."

"Same to you and your lovely parents." I think it strange she is calling me on a holiday. She must have others more important to her.

"I hope I'm not disturbing your day," she says.

"Oh, no, we'll have our main meal at noon. All my family is here and I've invited Lorene Perkins and Alicia Colby to join us."

She clears her throat. "The reason I called . . ."

I wait to hear awful news but I am dead wrong.

"Attorney Jacob Dunwoody phoned me yesterday," she begins. "Lloyd took out a million-dollar life insurance on himself three years ago—I suppose because he's in constant danger." She grabs a breath.

"I wasn't aware he has family," I recall.

"He doesn't. His mother Susan died several years ago."

I wonder why Ellie's sharing this information with me.

"Lloyd named me as his beneficiary."

Wow! I think, but words are stuck in my throat.

"I want to buy your farm. My parents will sell their home and move south with me," she explains. "Name your price."

I am overwhelmed and totally caught off balance.

"That's very generous of you, Ellie. Can I think about it?"

"Sure. We're in no hurry. Take your time. I know Claire would like to have you living closer to her in Nashville."

Because I am getting older, I finish her thought.

"Well, that is why I phoned, Dorothy. Let us know."

"I certainly will. And enjoy your day."

I end the call and walk into the dining room. The food is on my long walnut table that seats twelve people. Claire has set up a small table for my two great grandchildren, Billy and June. They are seated, their bright eyes watching me to signal it's time to eat. Bless them!

"Come sit down, Mama." Claire pulls out Arthur's captain chair at one end of the table. Her husband Ted sits at the opposite end.

"Thank you." I take a seat and feel honored. "Ted, would you say the blessing over our food for us?" I bow my head.

"Dearest Heavenly Father, we are so grateful to you for another year and the many blessings You bestow upon each of us. We're especially thankful Mama is fine and survived an assault on her life. Bless this meal as we honor Your Son's birth. Amen."

"Amen," we all say.

"Graham, will you serve the turkey?" I request.

"Yes, Mama. And thanks for your hospitality."

"You are most welcome, and congratulations on your marriage to Cynthia." I give her my best smile. "Welcome to our family, Cyn."

"Thank you, Mrs. Powell." She smiles sweetly.

Besides being super smart and our county coroner, Graham's wife is beautiful. Her golden-blond hair glistens in the den's bright lighting.

Lorene is loquacious today, upstaging Alicia's usual barrage of questions when she doesn't understand something about American culture. They could not be more different, and I love them both.

We laugh, tell jokes, rehash the year's events, and pig out on dessert last of all. Full and now sleepy, we bring the dishes into the kitchen and stack them. "Let's sit for a while," I suggest.

"Alicia and I will help Dorothy clean up later," Lorene states.

"Are you sure?" Claire asks, always bent on serving others.

"We're sure," all three of us answer then laugh.

Graham and Cynthia leave around two p.m., driving over to Murfreesboro to visit her parents and open presents. If they can squeeze one more portion of food in their stomachs, I'd be surprised.

Dusk fast approaches around four thirty. "We should go," Ted tells me as he wakes up from a long nap in my new recliner.

I get Claire's coat from the foyer closet while Ted snags his cap and jacket from the coat tree. "Why did Ellie call you?"

"She's offered to buy my farm," I reply.

"For how much?"

"She's receiving a million-dollar payout from Lloyd's life insurance policy," I explain. "She said name my price."

"Are you considering her offer?"

"I said I'd think about it." I really like living in Columbia, and I have such great friends. Lorene would be crushed.

"Oh, I almost forgot," Claire says.

"What?" I curiously look at her.

"This letter came for you." She hands me the envelope.

I stare at the postmark. *Moscow, Russia.*

"There must be a mistake," I tell Claire.

"No, the letter was in your mailbox."

"I picked up my mail yesterday," I tell her.

"Well, it must have come by Special Delivery."

I hold the letter, afraid to open it. Could it be a message from the Russian Mafia threatening my life? I stand there like a dumb bunny.

"Well, open the letter, Mama," Ted says. "We need to go."

I am shaking like a butterfly in a snowstorm as I slide a fingernail along the sticky edge on the back of the envelope. It's a card.

"What does it say, Mama?" Claire inquires.

"Merry Christmas!"

"Who sent it?"

"There's no signature." I show her.

"Who do you think it's from?" Ted asks.

I think of CIA secret agent Thomas Kessler.

Claire pulls me into the dining room, leaving Ted lingering in the foyer wondering what is going on. "Mama, is it from *him?*"

I know she refers to Tom.

"Did you sleep with him?"

I say nothing.

"Mama?"

A trip to Russia suddenly becomes appealing. If I sell my house, I will have plenty of money to travel all over the world. With him.

"Mama, answer me!" Claire demands.

"Claire! What happens undercover stays there."

www.ingramcontent.com/pod-product-compliance
Lightning Source LLC
Chambersburg PA
CBHW070042260626
47159CB00005B/2101